A JOYFUL SPRINGTIME AT ROOKERY HOUSE

ROSIE HENDRY

A Joyful Springtime at Rookery House

Copyright © 2025 by Rosie Hendry
ISBN: 978-1-914443-35-0

This is a work of fiction. All characters and events in this publication, other than those in the public domain, are fictitious and any resemblance to real persons, living or dead, is purely coincidental.

All rights reserved. No part of this publication may be reproduced, stored in a retrieval system, or transmitted, in any form or by any means, without the prior written permission of the publisher.

Published by Rookery House Press
Cover design by designforwriters.com

For David,
with love and thanks.

CHAPTER 1

Sussex, England – mid-April 1943

Genevieve Hamilton-Jones, otherwise known as Evie Jones, balanced one end of the wooden tray on her hip, freeing up a hand to open the greenhouse door. Stepping inside, she was met with warmth and the scents of rich, earthy soil and the greenery of tender growing seedlings.

'Hello, darling.' Evie's mother greeted her with a swift smile. She was sowing seeds, scattering them onto the surface of the compost-filled terracotta clay pot, one of several that stood on the long wooden bench running down one side of the large greenhouse. It was something her mother had done in this exact same way ever since Evie could remember and, watching her now, Evie was cast back through all the long years since her childhood.

She put the tray down in a space at the end of the bench. 'I thought you might like a drink – I have some of Mrs Haver's blackberry cordial.'

'Oh thank you! That's most thoughtful of you.' Her mother glanced at her gold wristwatch. 'Goodness, I'd quite lost track of time. But that always happens when I'm out here in my garden.' She gave a contented laugh. 'I do love it so.'

'I'm the same when I'm reading. I get so engrossed in a book that the outside world fades away for a while.' Evie picked up a glass of the rich pink cordial from the tray and held it out. 'Here you are.'

Her mother quickly wiped her soil-smudged hands down the front of her dun-coloured canvas apron before accepting the glass.

'Thank you.' She took a long drink. 'That was most welcome – so refreshing. It's getting quite warm in here, what with it being such a glorious spring day.'

'Mrs Haver's cordial is always delicious,' Evie agreed after taking a sip of her own drink, enjoying the fruity mellow flavour of her mother's cook's recipe. 'I took some to Mr Oakes and Ned too.'

Evie raised herself on to her tiptoes and looked out across the garden. She could see Ned and Mr Oakes talking and laughing while they took a break from digging over the vegetable beds, their now empty glasses still held loosely in their hands.

This morning wasn't the first time Ned had assisted the elderly gardener since he and Evie had arrived here from Norfolk five days ago. So much for Ned having a holiday from his gardening work at Great Plumstead Hall, Evie thought. Though it was Ned who'd offered to help and he was clearly enjoying spending time with Mr Oakes, who'd worked for Evie's parents for as long as she could remember and was now well past the age of retirement.

'I've tried to find help for Mr Oakes in the garden,' her mother said, following Evie's gaze. 'But with so many men away with the war, and women doing war work too, it's proved impossible. And he refuses to retire – he loves this garden quite as much as I do and I'm sure he doesn't ever want to leave me in the lurch. It's so kind of Ned to help him while he's here, especially when he's supposed to be having a break. I do appreciate it.'

'Ned loves it, don't worry about that,' Evie reassured her mother. 'Mr Oakes knows so much and Ned is always keen to learn, especially about the old ways and how things used to be done to keep a garden going, not just for a season but for generations. And besides, Ned and I have still had time each afternoon to do other things too. It's been a pleasure showing Ned around where I grew up.'

'Your visit has flown by. I do hope you'll come again soon.' Her mother's voice was wistful.

'It's been a joy to be back here. I always loved this house and garden.' Evie had sorely missed her home when she'd been sent away to boarding school when she was twelve years old.

Her mother took a step closer and put her hand on Evie's arm. 'It's been so wonderful to see you and have you back home again for a while. It was something I thought would never happen again after I was told you'd been killed in the Blitz.' She paused for a few moments, a troubled look clouding her face. 'I'll never forget the utter relief I felt when I got your letter telling me that you were alive.' Her mother's voice grew husky and she placed a hand to her chest. 'I know you could so easily have let me go on thinking you'd been killed. It's what I deserved. I didn't support or help you when you confessed to me how badly Douglas was treating you. I'm ashamed of how I behaved. I just wouldn't let myself think it could be true, not even when you showed me your bruises and told me about your miscarriage. I wouldn't believe it of him.'

Her eyes shimmered with tears. 'I'm so terribly sorry that I failed you when you needed me.'

Evie nodded, laying her hand over her mother's. 'It was a horrible time but it's in the past. Douglas is gone and can never hurt me again. It might help to remember that you weren't the only one he fooled – he was extremely good at hiding his real character and charming people. He deceived me too before we were married. It was only afterwards that he allowed his mask to slip and revealed the real Douglas. By then it was too late for me. I'd made my vows to him and I foolishly hoped and kept on hoping that he would change.' Evie let out a heavy sigh. 'But he didn't change. I don't think he ever would have, even if he'd survived the war.' She raised her chin and met her mother's eyes. 'But I'm extremely happy now. I love my job as a nurse and I love Ned! I've found a real, good man who's more of a gentleman than Douglas could ever have been.'

Her mother glanced out at Ned again before returning her gaze to Evie. 'He's a lovely young man. I like him very much, but is it *serious* between you, darling? More than just a wartime romance?'

'It's serious,' Evie said, her voice firm. 'I love him. He's intelligent, kind, caring and thoughtful.'

'I can see that, darling. There's no disputing any of those admirable traits, but where do you think your romance with him might lead? Or are you just living for the day like so many young people do these days with this dreadful war on?' Her mother's voice was deceptively light, but there was an uncertain look in her eyes. 'And who can blame them because no one knows what tomorrow will bring – even if any of us will still be here. This war isn't mostly taking place in distant countries like during the Great War. This time it's come right up to our doorsteps. We've seen so much of it going on right over our heads every time our brave fighter pilot boys come up against enemy planes.' She waved her hand towards the sky.

Evie looked down at her feet, nudging at a stone on the brown, earthen floor of the greenhouse with the toe of her shoe. She'd been expecting her mother to bring this up at some point during their stay, to question Evie about her intentions. Now, with Evie and Ned due to leave after lunch, Evie needed to be crystal clear with her mother about this, while they were on their own and wouldn't be overheard. There must be no confusion.

She met her mother's eyes and spoke in a calm voice. 'As far as I'm concerned Ned is going to be part of my life, a very important part, till the end of my days. Unless of course my judgement is faulty and I've put my faith in the wrong man again. But I *very much* doubt Ned will prove to be an ill choice. Not from what I know and have seen of him. Ned is steadfast and true. I don't think there is a hidden side to him like there was with Douglas.'

'You're not thinking of marriage, are you?' Her mother's voice rose slightly, a concerned look on her face. 'Only, if you were thinking of marrying Ned, well...' She hesitated for a moment. 'He's not the sort of man your father and I would have expected you to marry. Nice as Ned may be, he's a gardener's son and now a gardener himself. He...'

Evie put her palm out to stop her mother, fixing her with a firm stare. 'I really don't care that Ned is a gardener or what his father or even his grandfather did for a living or how much money they earned. Life has taught me a hard lesson that it's *not* the social class someone comes from or how much money someone has that makes them a good and decent person. It's their character and whether they have a good heart and kindness woven into their soul. Douglas was wealthy and had high social standing but he was woefully lacking when it came to the important characteristics that would have made him a good and decent person, let alone a loving and caring husband. You really must stop judging people by status and money, Mother. They mean *nothing*.'

'It's how I was brought up. What I was educated to believe,' her mother said in a wounded voice, folding her arms across the front of her apron.

'But that doesn't mean you have to follow that any more and carry on thinking that way. The world is changing. Surely what happened to me has proven that narrow view to be misguided.' Evie softened her voice. 'Just so you know, I have no intention of *ever* legally getting married again,' she said, truthfully. 'I won't ever put myself in that situation again for anyone – not even for Ned. And he knows that. He understands.'

'Then he is a most understanding man,' her mother said, holding Evie's gaze.

Evie bit her lip. Her mother was regarding her closely. Now was the time to tell her. The whole truth and nothing but the truth.

'We're going to *pretend* to be married.' There, she'd said it. Her mother's eyes widened in alarm as Evie rushed on, 'We'll live together, without being legally tied. When we go back to Great Plumstead, it will be as a married couple, after apparently "marrying" while we were away. So people will assume. And we won't contradict them.'

Her mother shook her head. 'Genevieve, that's lying! And… not the way things should be! Living together when you're not married… it's just not done!'

'No, it's not done. At least, not very often.'

'Then you agree with me. That it's not right.'

'I do not. Just because something isn't the done thing

doesn't mean it's not the *right* thing. The very *best* thing in some circumstances. And this is the best thing for me. After all that I've been through...'

Evie felt her words catch in her throat as a dark wave of emotion threatened to crash over her. Douglas, her years married, his abuse... she shivered, and let those old feelings pass by. That time was over. Now she had a chance of a life she'd barely been brave enough to even dream of.

Evie's mother was staring at her. At least she's still here, Evie thought. She hasn't stormed away. Or told me to leave, to get out, and never darken her doorway again...

'I wanted to tell *you* the truth, Mother. Not lie to *you*,' Evie said. 'That's why I came here.'

Her mother was frowning. Her gardener's hands were entwined tightly at her chest.

'The only reason we must pretend to be married is because so many people would judge us badly for not conforming to the normal way of doing things. The people in Great Plumstead, the villagers ... they're not unkind, in fact they're quite the opposite. But I expect a number of them would find it difficult, if they knew we lived together and were unmarried.'

'They would,' her mother said quietly. 'Of course they would.'

'Ned might lose his job. We might have to move away from the life I've built there. Rookery House. My friends.'

Her mother nodded but gave no other sign.

'I took the conventional way before, with Douglas, and I bitterly regretted it. This time I want to be with someone I love on my terms. And if that requires pretending – *lying* – then so be it.'

She took her mother's hands in hers.

'You are my mother. I was hoping that you would give us

your support. That you would value my happiness more than what's considered the proper way to do things.'

Evie could see the conflict of emotions playing on her mother's face and was uncertain what her response was going to be. The conventions her mother lived by had taught her that Ned was beneath Evie as a match. Accepting even that was a huge leap for her mother to take. And so the idea her daughter was about to live a lie… Evie was sure that was a step too far.

Her mother's eyes were bright with tears. 'You have my support and my word that I will keep your secret. I once let you down and I won't ever do that again. What you're doing is *unconventional* but as you say the world is changing and we must change with it.' She wrapped her arms around Evie and hugged her tightly.

Evie hugged her back thinking she hadn't felt such closeness to her mother since she was a very small child.

'I wish you both much happiness together,' her mother whispered. 'You and Ned have my utmost blessing.'

Evie would have enjoyed her mother's embrace for longer, but the sound of feet crunching on the gravel path towards the greenhouse made her mother let go.

'Thank you,' she told her mother, as Ned arrived at the door.

'Mrs Havers has said that lunch will be ready in twenty minutes at half past twelve. I need to go and finish my packing before then,' Ned explained. 'So I'm heading back indoors.'

'I'll come as I have things to pack too,' Evie told him.

Leaving her mother in the greenhouse, Evie headed back to the house, hand in hand with Ned and happy that she'd done the right thing and told her mother the truth. Her mother had given Evie her full support and there was a new warmth between them. It mattered to Evie that the important people in her life knew what she and Ned were doing. They were her mother and those closest to her at Rookery House – Thea, Hettie, Flo and Marianne, all of whom she considered her family and could trust whenever life got too tough to handle on her own.

∼

After saying their goodbyes at the house, Evie led Ned back to the village station where they left their luggage so they could take one last walk before beginning their return journey.

Evie was excited. She had saved her favourite place in the village till last and was so very much looking forward to sharing it with Ned.

'It's time the two of you finally met,' Evie said, with a grin.

'I can hardly wait,' said Ned, taking her hand.

The wood was filled with magnificent beech trees. Nestling to one side of the village, it was a place she'd walked to often, enjoying it in every season of the year. Even in autumn, when its paths were littered with copper, russet and golden leaves that crunched underfoot, and deepest winter, when the trees became stately grey-trunked sleeping giants, the wood was never anything less than enchanting. But in springtime...

'Ah!' Evie heard Ned gasp at the sight before them. 'That is so beautiful.'

'It's just as I remember it!'

With spring bursting forth, the floor of the wood was covered with a vista of flowering bluebells that stretched away in a hazy blue carpet as far as they could see. Evie breathed in the delicate scent of the flowers and let out a soft sigh of contentment.

'I'm so glad you could see the wood like this. Isn't it

marvellous? I love how each flower combines to make this whole...' she threw her arms out wide, 'spectacle! It's glorious! Heavenly!'

'It is,' Ned agreed. She detected an odd note in his voice and looked at him quizzically, but he responded with a laugh. 'It really is,' he said. 'Glorious and heavenly.'

Evie squeezed his arm then crouched down and gently touched a cluster of blue bell-like flowers hanging from the bowed top of a green stem. She watched as a bumble bee hovered close to her hand for a moment, before speeding off on the breeze.

She stood up and put her arm through Ned's. 'Let's walk.'

They followed a path that wove through the wood with the haze of bluebells stretching off on either side. It was a delight for the senses, Evie thought, from the colour and aroma of the flowers to the singing of birds and buzzing of bees. An English springtime at its best. Strangely, Ned didn't seem to be enjoying it as much as she was.

'Are you all right, Ned?' Evie asked, glancing at him. 'You're very quiet.'

'I'm... just thinking about what we're about to do. Our Plan.' He stopped and turned to face her, his face serious. 'I need to talk to you about it.'

Evie's stomach twisted, as her instincts told her something was awry. 'What is it?'

'It's about our marriage. Our pretend marriage.' Ned's eyes met hers.

'But we talked about it and... you *agreed* to it. We even bought the ring in Norwich on our way here.'

'I know. I've got it here.' Ned patted the chest pocket of his jacket. 'Yes, you're right I did agree to it, but now...'

'You're having second thoughts? After we've come this far?'

The prospect made her feel ill. 'You know why I can't marry you legally, Ned. I just can't.'

Had her chance at happiness with Ned been only a dream after all? Was their plan to live a lie simply too much for him to bear?

'It was when I saw the bluebells,' Ned said and his eyes took on a faraway look as he gazed around them. 'Look at us, we're like an island in a sea of blue.'

'And that's made you not want to be with me?' Evie said, incredulously.

Ned looked horrified. 'No! It's only made me want that even more! I want *more*, Evie. Here in this wood, amongst the glorious bluebells – I want to…' He took hold of her hands in his. 'I want to make a promise to you.'

'A promise?'

'Like I would have done in a church or registry office. I think…' He looked around them for a moment before returning his attention to her. 'This beautiful place that means so much to you is the right place to make my promise.'

He peered into her face so earnestly she laughed. 'Ned Blythe, you are such a romantic!'

'You know, maybe I am! So what do you think? Could you tolerate this romantic fool of a man declaring his love and promise to you amongst a sea of bluebells?'

Evie beamed. 'I think I'd rather like that.'

Ned dropped down onto his knees, still holding her hands in his. 'Evie, I promise you with all my heart that I will love, care and be true to you for the rest of my days.' He spoke each word with meaning, his eyes full of love for her. 'No matter what life throws at us, I will *always* be steadfastly by your side.'

Evie's eyes filled with tears as Ned's declaration touched her heart. She hadn't expected this to happen, and especially here of all places, but it was perfect! He released her hands, reached into his jacket pocket and took out a small, black square box. He opened it to reveal a plain gold wedding ring. They'd bought it at a jewellers shop in Norwich when they'd walked across the city between railway stations on their way to Sussex. The plan was for Evie to be wearing it on their return to Great Plumstead having apparently married while they were in Sussex, making their pretend marriage credible.

Ned took the ring from the box and carefully slipped it onto the fourth finger of Evie's left hand. 'This is a token of my love for you and my promise to you.'

Evie looked at the ring. It glinted in the sunshine filtering down through the trees and seemed tinged with the colour of bluebells.

'Thank you.' Her eyes met Ned's and she pulled him up to standing. 'I promise to love and care for you to the end of my days.' They were simple words but Evie said them with sincerity, meaning every single one with all her heart and soul. 'I hadn't thought we would do something like this but I'm so glad we have. Thank you.' Evie kissed him and held him in a tight embrace.

'The trees are our witnesses,' said Ned, 'there's no need for anyone else.'

She glanced up at the tall beech trees whose high branches overhead made a cathedral-like roof to the wood.

'I feel like you're my wife and I'm your husband now,' Ned said as they slowly loosened their hold and stood looking at each other, their hands on each other's arms. 'We don't need a legal ceremony because what we said to each other is the important bit, and keeping our words and being true to our promises for the rest of our lives. That's what matters.'

Ned picked a single bluebell stem and handed it to her. 'For you.'

'Thank you,' Evie said, taking it and holding it up to her

face to breath in the perfume. 'I'll press it and keep it as a reminder of today.'

'I'd pick you a whole bunch of bluebells but they don't last well,' Ned said.

'I tried that as a child and was always disappointed by how quickly they wilted.' Evie rested her head on his shoulder and Ned wrapped his arm around her. 'Best to admire and enjoy them while they're here. I think that's one of the reasons bluebells are so special.'

As they stood quietly together, Evie felt as if they had stepped into a new phase of their lives. They'd had their wedding ceremony, just between the pair of them and the wood, saying what was important to each other. It was personal, real, honest and about their love for each other.

'As much as I would like to stay here, we have a train to catch,' Evie said reluctantly a few minutes later. 'Come on, husband of mine,' she grinned at him and linked her arm through his. 'Let our married life begin!'

As they walked arm in arm, back to the village station, Evie felt lighter, her heart warm with happiness. They were stopping in Suffolk rather than going straight back to Great Plumstead, spending two nights in a country hotel which would now become their honeymoon suite. With such a beautiful start to their unofficial married life she hoped with all her heart that her and Ned's relationship would continue to blossom. This time it felt utterly different, not just because they'd made their promises under the canopy of a beech wood rather than in a flower-decked church. The crucial difference was in the man – in her beloved Ned.

CHAPTER 2

The Mother's Day Club Workroom, Great Plumstead – Norfolk.

Prue Wilson finished sewing on the last button to complete the boy's shirt and tied it off with a secure knot. She knew from her own experience as a mother just how much tugging shirt buttons often had to withstand when shirts were taken off by their young wearers.

Other members from The Mother's Day Club were making garments for the village clothing depot. Founder member, Gloria Jessop, was busy at the hand-cranked sewing machine, stitching pieces of flower-printed fabric together to make a girl's dress, the machine's gentle hum providing a background accompaniment to the chatter of the other women as they worked.

Looking around her, Prue still marvelled at how the room had been transformed into such a cheerful and productive place. These days it was often occupied by women who'd dropped in to work on something for the clothing depot, mend clothes, or darn socks for the RAF airmen at the local aerodrome. It was totally unrecognisable from this time last year, Prue thought. Back then, it was a study for the sole use of her late husband Victor. It had been a dull, drab place, where he'd pored over his accounts, keeping an over-zealous eye on the pounds, shillings and pence earned by his business. Prue only ever ventured in when summoned by Victor, and then she would have to endure him moaning at her about something she'd done that wasn't to his taste or didn't suit his opinion. Every visit to Victor's study had been an unpleasant experience for Prue.

All that was now changed for the better. The room had been painted a cheerful pink, new curtains put up, the wooden parquet floor exposed and polished. The shelves which once held weighty ledgers and accounts books were now stocked with colourful yarn and fabric.

This dramatic change had only been possible because Victor was gone. He'd been killed at the end of last April during the Norwich Blitz while visiting his mistress. Prue didn't miss him all. Even if he hadn't had a mistress, she'd have felt the same way because her marriage had never been a happy one. It was only ever one of convenience. Victor had married her so he had someone to look after his two small sons, Jack and Edwin, after their mother had died. As for Prue, she'd married Victor because she'd believed it was her only chance to be a mother, with so many eligible men of her age lost in the Great War.

Prue had thought they might eventually grow closer, but the truth was there'd never been any real affection between her and Victor over the years. The arrival of their daughter Alice had been the best thing to come from their marriage alongside Prue's mothering of her step-sons. But instead of

Prue and Victor becoming at least a partnership in the upbringing of the children, he had controlled and dominated their home, often making it an unhappy place to live. It was a relief that he was gone, Prue thought, and not for the first time. The removal of Victor had given Prue a brighter future and a new lease of life – just like this vibrant new workroom.

'Anyone fancy a cuppa?' Prue asked, pushing thoughts of Victor firmly into the past where they belonged.

'Yes please!' Gloria called, followed by a chorus of the same from the other women.

'I won't be long.' Prue quickly folded the shirt and put it on the pile of other garments ready to be taken to the clothes depot, then headed into the kitchen.

She'd put the kettle on to boil and was setting out cups on a tray when she heard a knock at the front door. Hurrying down the hall to answer it, Prue was surprised to see who was standing on the doorstep – it was Lady Campbell-Gryce.

'Hello!' Prue greeted her friend. 'Have you come to do some sewing? There are quite a few of us working this morning but there's always room for more to join in.'

'Good morning, Prue, I can't I'm afraid. Not today,' her Ladyship replied. 'I want to ask you something. I need your help.'

'Of course, come in and I'll help you if I can,' Prue said as sounds of laughter came down the hall from the workroom.

'Not here, I need to speak to you in private.' An anxious expression washed over Lady Campbell-Gryce's face. 'It's a rather sensitive matter, you see.'

Prue nodded. In the past year the two women, though from different social backgrounds, had got to know each other and had both shared secrets, keeping those confidences to themselves. Prue appreciated that whatever her friend had to say would be best said out of possible earshot of anyone else, even the trustworthy members of The Mother's Day Club working in the workroom.

'Of course. Can you give me a moment? I was just making the tea. Then shall we take a walk down to the river?' Prue suggested. 'It will be quiet down there.'

'That sounds ideal.' Lady Campbell-Gryce gave Prue a grateful smile. 'I'll wait out here for you.'

Returning to the kitchen, where the kettle was coming to the boil, Prue quickly poured hot water into the teapot. Then she put it on the tray with the cups and jug of milk and carried it into the workroom.

'I've got to pop out for a bit,' Prue told Gloria. 'Can I leave this with you?'

'Right you are, ducks,' Gloria said. 'I'll keep an eye on things for you 'ere. Is everything all right?'

'Yes, everything's fine. I just need to go and do something.' Prue patted Gloria's arm, then went out into the hallway, grabbed her jacket from the stand and let herself out of the front door.

Outside, Lady Campbell-Gryce was admiring the clumps of daffodils growing in Prue's front garden, their golden yellow flowers dancing in the April breeze.

'I do so love daffodils,' her Ladyship said as Prue opened the front gate and gestured for her friend to go through ahead of her. 'Golden stars of brightness after the dark winter days. They make one's spirits rise.'

'They're such cheerful flowers,' Prue agreed. 'We need that burst of brilliance after the drabness of winter.'

As they made their way down to where the River Bure ran through the village, they chatted about what the women were working on in the workroom. All the while though, Prue was wondering what she could possibly do to help her Ladyship. Prue was used to being asked to find homes for evacuees, or organise things for the WVS or WI – she was, she had to admit, someone people trusted to solve those kinds of problems and minor emergencies. Lady Campbell-Gryce, by contrast, always seemed more than capable of handling whatever life sent her way, without needing anybody's help. It was her Ladyship's air of confidence and self-control that Prue most admired about her.

'The river's running high after all that rain over the past few days,' Lady Campbell-Gryce commented as they reached the riverbank and came to a halt, watching the mud-coloured water flowing past at a faster rate than usual. She turned to face Prue. 'I'm sure you're wondering what's going on and why I need your help. Do you remember last year I told you that Lord Campbell-Gryce, Anthony, has had a string of mistresses right from when we first married?'

Prue nodded as she recalled the day she'd been heading back down the drive from Great Plumstead Hall after her first delivery of Rural Pie Scheme pies to the gardeners. She'd met her Ladyship, who had asked how Prue was coping following Victor's death. Without thinking, Prue had blurted out that Victor had been with his mistress when he'd been killed. To Prue's astonishment, Lady Campbell-Gryce had admitted that her own husband had mistresses.

Their shared confidences had been the start of a friendship which had brought her Ladyship more into the village community. She'd even joined in with the women of The Mother's Day Club, helping to set up the workroom and spending time there sewing or knitting.

'I do remember,' Prue confirmed. 'You told me about Anthony after I confessed about Victor. Has something happened?'

'Not yet, but I believe there's a real danger that it could. I've never been bothered about Anthony's mistresses before –

as far as I was concerned, they were quite welcome to him. None of them have ever been a threat. He's never been serious about any of them; they've just been a distraction, a flirtation and temporary fling until he grew bored and moved on to the next one. But now...' She paused, pressing her lips into a thin line for a moment before continuing, 'A reliable source has warned me that this time it's different. Anthony is apparently smitten with the latest one and I fear it is serious. From what I hear, this woman won't be satisfied until she is his wife.'

Prue gave a small gasp before recovering her composure. 'How would you feel about that?' she asked gently.

'It's not happening while I'm alive!' Lady Campbell-Gryce's cheeks bloomed with pink spots. 'I've put a lot of my life and effort into Great Plumstead Hall, always ignoring Anthony's affairs until now. I've made sure our children are happy. I was always the one who bothered and cared about Cecelia and Henry, made them a seemingly happy home. My dowry which came with me when Anthony and I married, helped shore up the estate and kept it going strong. Without my money it's likely the estate would have had to be sold off, the way so many other families have had to do. The point is that I have turned a blind eye to Anthony's other women, but I can't do the same with this one. I need to act and soon. He needs reminding of what he stands to lose.'

'You want me to help you do that?' Prue asked, puzzled at how she could intervene with Lord Campbell-Gryce, a man she'd never even spoken to before.

'I want you to come with me to York.'

'York?' Prue frowned. 'Why there?'

'That's where he's meeting her next week. I want to catch him there and make him see sense.'

Prue didn't know what to say and tried hurriedly to gather her thoughts.

'I want you to be there, Prue, to witness what's going on. I know I can trust you to be discreet if things should go awry. I will pay all your expenses and we'd stay with my friend Caroline. She heard what was going on and alerted me to the danger. It's her cousin's daughter who's involved with Anthony and her cousin's quite delighted – she would love her daughter to become the next Lady Campbell-Gryce. Her cousin doesn't know that Caroline and I are old friends going back to our school days. York isn't far from where your daughter is stationed. You could see Alice while we are there. What do you say, will you help me Prue, please?'

'Of course I will help.' Prue's mind was already planning ahead, as it always was when there was a problem to solve for somebody. 'I'll need to arrange cover for my shifts at The Mother's Day Club, on the WVS canteen and my Rural Pie Scheme delivery, but that shouldn't be a problem.'

Lady Campbell-Gryce closed her eyes briefly and when she opened them again, Prue saw their blueness was enhanced by a sheen of tears.

'Thank you so much. I'll feel a good deal braver with you by my side. I honestly don't know if this will work or not, but I'm not going down without a fight.'

'I hope it works out for you,' Prue said.

Her Ladyship raised her chin. 'So do I. And no matter what, we shall have a lovely time visiting York and staying with Caroline. She's a darling. Have you been to York before?'

'Never, but Alice has written about it in her letters. She says the Minster is beautiful. I'd very much like to see that.'

'Then you shall,' Lady Campbell-Gryce said. 'I'm sure you'll love it; it's different to Norwich's cathedral, York's Minster is huge and quite spectacular. Now, is there any sewing I can help with in the workroom?'

Prue let out a laugh. 'Always! Come on, let's get back and

you can have some tea and join in. You're always most welcome.'

'I enjoy working in there when I can and my sewing skills are measuredly improved from what they were. Thank you again, Prue, for agreeing to come to York with me. I'll let you know all the details, date, times and such soon if that's all right?'

'Of course.' Prue put her hand on her friend's arm. 'You're not alone in this.'

'Thank you. I appreciate that so much. You are one of the few people I know I can be sure of with this matter.'

'You can trust me,' Prue reassured her. 'I know how hard it is to keep secrets thrust on us by our husband's behaviour. They are imposed on us whether we like it or not and that's why we must do all we can to stop them ruining our lives. Come on, let's go and do some mending. There'll be plenty of chatter and laughter to help take your mind off things for a little while.'

As they made their way back to her house, Prue couldn't help thinking how you never knew what was around the corner. Only a short while ago she'd been sewing on buttons and now here she was planning a trip to York, a place she'd never been, to help her friend and have a chance to see Alice. Life was full of surprises!

CHAPTER 3

What a difference compared to her first visit here a little over a year ago, Hettie thought as she rode her bicycle down the track to Crossways Farm. On that occasion she'd had to carefully steer a safe path around the many dips and bumps that riddled the track to avoid being jarred off her bicycle. Now the potholes had been filled in and she could ride smoothly and safely along, taking time to admire the clumps of butter-yellow primroses growing in the shelter of the hedgerow banks lining the lane.

She was out this afternoon doing one of her regular visits as Great Plumstead's local Land Army Representative – a role she'd been asked to do last year and which she thoroughly enjoyed. Today she was popping into Crossways Farm to check on Iris, who'd been working here as a Land Girl since last May and had settled in well and was making a difference to the farm.

Steering her bicycle into the farmyard, Hettie came to a halt and dismounted, leaning her bike against the wall enclosing the farmhouse's small front garden. She was halfway up the path to the front door when it was opened by Beattie Southgate, who welcomed her with a beaming smile.

'Afternoon, Hettie, you've got perfect timing. I've just made a pot of tea. Come you on in. Iris knows you're expected this afternoon and said she'll be in to see you.'

'Thank you, Beattie.' Hettie followed the farmer's wife into the house and closed the front door behind her.

Heading into the farmhouse kitchen, which was warmed by heat from the black iron stove just like the one at Rookery House, Hettie was met by the delicious aroma of freshly baked bread. Two loaves were upside down cooling on a metal rack on the table standing in the middle of the room.

'The bread smells delicious,' Hettie said. 'It's one of my favourite things to make.'

Beattie's mouth fell open. 'I'd never have expected a former cook from the Hall to say that, not with all your fancy cooking skills and experience. To say you like baking bread the best. I'd never have guessed!' She gestured for Hettie to sit down at the table while she poured out two cups of tea from the teapot and passed one over to Hettie.

Hettie laughed. 'It's true. I always enjoy the whole process of bread making. Mixing the dough, leaving it to rise, the kneading. The smell after it's cooked. In my opinion it's often the simplest things that are the best. You know, if you offered me a choice of some of the fancy foods I used to cook for a grand dinner at the Hall, or a simple meal of freshly baked bread, cheese and a home-grown tomato, warmed by the sun, then I'd choose the simple meal.'

'I'm the same,' said Beattie. 'Good honest grub is what I like and what I cook here at the farm.'

Hettie took a sip of her tea then asked, 'How are things with Iris?'

'All good, she seems happy and is still enjoying the work. I like having her here and so does Stan – though you wouldn't get him to admit it!' Beattie looked amused.

'And to think he thought the girl should sleep out in the barn!' Hettie said, thinking of her first visit to Crossways Farm when she'd been sent by the Land Army office in Norwich to check the arrangements for a potential Land Girl were suitable.

Stan Southgate had showed Hettie up a flight of rickety stairs in a barn to a cobweb-festooned upper floor where she'd been able to see the sky through gaps in the tiles. Hettie had told him immediately – and with some outrage – that it most definitely wasn't suitable for a Land Girl. Thankfully, Beattie had been on hand to offer a much better bedroom in the farmhouse and Hettie had approved the accommodation.

Beattie raised her eyebrows, shaking her head. 'I was so embarrassed! Stan just wouldn't listen to me when I told him that old barn wasn't any good. It took your reaction to bring him to his senses. Still, it's all worked out …' She halted as the door leading into the scullery, and out to the back door of the farmhouse, opened and a young woman walked in. She was dressed in Land Army corduroy trousers and a green jumper and had her blonde, curly hair mostly covered with a scarf.

'Hello!' Iris greeted Hettie warmly.

'Lovely to see you, Iris. You're looking well.'

Iris pulled out a chair and sat down at the table. 'All this fresh country air is making me rosy.' She put her hands to her cheeks which had a much healthier glow compared with when she'd first arrived to work here from her home in Nottingham. 'I'm so glad I escaped working in a factory. Being stuck inside all day didn't suit me at all!'

'We're lucky to have you,' Beattie said, passing Iris the cup of tea she'd just poured her.

Hettie gave a small sigh of satisfaction as she watched the

young woman smile back at the farmer's wife. There was clearly a bond of affection between them and Hettie was glad things had worked out so well here for all of them – Iris, Beattie and Stan Southgate. Seeing how things developed and changed with the arrival of Land Girls on farms that were struggling, with so many men away because of the war, was one of the joys of doing this job. And it made her proud to be a small part of it.

CHAPTER 4

Marianne checked the pattern piece was correctly aligned along the grain of the pale blue fabric, then began to pin the paper securely in place. She was in the dining room at Rookery House this afternoon, using the large table to spread out the fabric as it gave her plenty of space to work.

As she pinned, she thought of the many garments she'd made over the years for people from all walks of life. Ball gowns, wedding dresses, formal suits fit for a Lady… and yet this simple shirt was getting more of her care and attention than anything else. And that was because it was for someone she cared for more than anything else, apart from her adorable children of course. This shirt was for Alex, her husband.

Marianne smiled, seeing his handsome face in her mind's eye, always beaming back at her.

'Oh, Alex,' she said aloud. 'This is for you, my dear, from your darling wife.'

Making this shirt was one of the few ways she could do something for him, and using her skills and expertise to make it as perfect as she could was one way of communicating her feelings for him. She would sew every stitch with love, pouring her devotion to him into the simple garment. With Alex incarcerated in a Prisoner of War camp somewhere in Germany, there was no possibility of Marianne seeing him, or even having the chance to speak to him on the telephone. Their only means of contact were the letters they exchanged and the next-of-kin parcels that she was permitted to send him four times a year. This shirt was to go in the next parcel, which she'd be sending to him in June.

Finishing pinning the last pattern piece, Marianne did a final check that everything was correct, before picking up her dressmaking scissors and starting to cut through the fabric. Her scissors made a satisfying snip each time the two blades sliced through the material and came together. She'd been pleased to find this fabric in the haberdashery in Wykeham, knowing it would make a good shirt – although how long it would take her to complete, Marianne couldn't be sure. These days her free time to sew without interruption was limited – she had three-year-old Emily and one-year-old Bea to look after. Marianne could only snatch spare moments, usually while her daughters were having an afternoon nap.

The sudden ringing of the telephone out in the hall made Marianne start. She hoped that it wouldn't wake the girls. They'd not long gone down, tired after their busy morning out at The Mother's Day Club, and should sleep for at least an hour but not if they were woken by the ringing. Dashing out of the dining room, Marianne hurried along the hall to answer the phone. Hettie had gone out on one of her Land Army Representative visits, leaving just her and the girls inside the house.

Grabbing the receiver, she spoke into it, 'Rookery House.'

She expected it was someone for Thea, who was outside working in the garden.

'Hello,' a plummy voice came down the line. 'I'm hoping to speak to Mrs Fordham. Mrs Marianne Fordham.'

'Speaking, I'm Marianne.' She didn't recognise the voice. It wasn't Lady Campbell-Gryce. Was it one of her Ladyship's friends, wanting a garment designed for them like Marianne had done several times for her Ladyship?

'Oh Marianne! How lovely to speak to you. It's Marguerite.' Before Marianne had time to realise precisely who the woman was she added, 'Alex's sister!'

A heaviness settled in Marianne's stomach. The last time she'd had dealings with any of Alex's family it hadn't gone well. She'd been heavily pregnant with Bea and worried sick about Alex who'd been posted as Missing In Action, and she'd had no idea whether he was dead or alive.

Without any warning at all, Alex's mother had turned up at Rookery House, but rather than coming to offer assistance or compassion to her son's wife and children, one still yet to be born, Mrs Fordham senior had immediately made matters even worse for Marianne. Having already decided that Alex was dead, Mrs Fordham had informed Marianne that, after the baby was born, she would return and take it and Emily to live with her and Alex's father. Her mother-in-law had said she wanted them brought up properly, which she'd scathingly declared Marianne was incapable of doing without a home of her own or a job. The older woman had shown no consideration for what Marianne wanted – which certainly wasn't to hand her children over to her mother-in-law's care. Especially as she'd informed Marianne that Alex's old nanny would be coming out of retirement to look after them so there'd be little grandparental love or affection. Marianne would have fought against that with every ounce of her strength.

Thankfully Mrs Fordham's threat to take the children had come to nothing as news came through that Alex was being kept as a POW for the remainder of the war. He might be in a camp with his liberty restricted, but he was alive! He'd survived his plane going down and one day, when the war was over, he would come home to them and they could be together as a family.

Marianne remembered her relief that the news of Alex had sent the dreaded Mrs Fordham packing and she had been further delighted not to have heard from her, or any of Alex's family, since.

Now, hearing from Alex's sister had instantly put Marianne on her guard. Was Marguerite acting on behalf of her mother – trying once more to take Emily and Bea from Marianne?

'Marianne, are you still there?' Marguerite's voice came again.

'Yes, I'm here.'

'Excellent. I'm ringing to tell you I've just been posted to a base on the Norfolk coast – can't say where of course, got to keep mum as they say, loose lips sink ships and all that!' She giggled.

'Alex told me in a letter that you'd joined the Wrens.'

'That's right and I'm loving it. It's jolly hard work but such fun too. Makes my life before I joined up seem rather drab and unfulfilled.' Marguerite's voice was thoughtful.

Marianne bit back a retort that her sister-in-law had had a very privileged life. Marguerite was a good friend of Cecilia Campbell-Gryce and had accompanied Cecilia to a fitting at Dorothy Abrahams dress designers in London where Marianne worked. That's when Marianne had first met her.

Naturally Marguerite hadn't taken much notice of Marianne then, no doubt regarding her as just a worker at the designers.

It was when Marguerite was having an evening gown made at Dorothy Abrahams that Marianne met Alex. He'd arranged to meet his sister after her fitting but, because it was taking longer than expected, he'd come in to wait for her and had talked to Marianne while she was working on his sister's dress. Afterwards he'd asked Marianne if she'd like to have some tea with him, but she'd refused, knowing her boss wouldn't have approved. But Alex hadn't been put off. He'd met her after work the next day and asked again, and that time she'd accepted his invitation. They'd begun a loving relationship that had faced several huge challenges along the way but they'd eventually married and now had two lovely children.

'I was thinking,' Marguerite's voice broke into Marianne's thoughts, 'that as I'm not far away from where you live now, it would be simply wonderful to come over to meet my two nieces. And see you of course.'

Panic flared in Marianne's chest. 'When?'

'Oh, I can't tell you that yet!' Marguerite laughed. 'My life is no longer my own, but I'll come and visit when I have some time off. I'll come on the train unless I can cadge a lift with someone. Petrol rationing is such a nuisance but we must all do our bit. Anyway, if it's fine with you, I'd like very much to visit and can let you know as soon as I have some leave. Listen I must go, there's a queue for the phone and I'm getting a hurry up signal from the next Wren who's desperate to telephone her chap. Lovely to talk to you Marianne. Look forward to seeing you and the girls. Bye for now!'

Before Marianne could reply the line went dead. She slowly replaced the black Bakelite receiver, feeling as if a whirlwind had hit her. Was Marguerite's intended visit purely to meet Emily and Bea and see her? Or was there another motive? Was she coming to spy on them for Marianne's mother-in-law? Check if the girls were being looked after properly. She let out a heavy sigh. Her sister-in-law hadn't given her any contact details, so Marianne had no way of getting in touch with her. All she could do was wait to hear from her again. Wait and worry.

Looking up the stairs, Marianne listened for any noise from the girls, but thankfully all was quiet. They'd slept through and not been disturbed by the telephone ringing. How much longer the peace would last, Marianne couldn't say – she'd better get back to her sewing and make the most of the time she had.

Though now while she worked, her thoughts of Alex were troubled with worries about his family – and how she must protect her girls from them.

CHAPTER 5

'They're here!'

Evie heard the joyful voice call out as she opened the back door of Rookery House and she and Ned went in. It was Sunday evening and they'd caught the train back to Great Plumstead after a glorious honeymoon in Woodbridge. Now they were returning to the village in their new role as *newlyweds*.

'Welcome home!' Thea hurried across the kitchen to meet them. Looking from Evie to Ned and back again, she tentatively asked, 'Are congratulations in order?'

'They are indeed!' Evie glanced at Ned who took hold of her left hand and held it up to show Thea, along with Hettie, Flo and Marianne who'd all gathered around, the golden band on Evie's fourth finger. With it being after seven o'clock all the children had gone to bed – Marianne's two daughters and Thea's evacuees, seven-year-old George and nine-year-old Betty.

'Excellent! Many congratulations! I'm so happy for you both.' Thea threw her arms around Evie and hugged her tightly, and then did the same to Ned.

More congratulations and hugs followed from the rest of Evie's gathered friends. Each of them knew that there'd been no *official* wedding, but that Evie and Ned loved each other and were committed to one another as much as any couple getting married in a church or registry office.

It had all started last December when Ned had surprised Evie by proposing to her, but as much as she loved him, she couldn't accept his offer. It was Thea who'd come up with a solution, suggesting they have a pretend marriage. She knew a couple who'd been unable to marry but who lived as a married couple and were extremely happy – not needing an official ceremony to show their love and commitment to each other. It was the perfect answer for Evie and Ned too.

Although their close and trusted friends here at Rookery House knew the truth, to everyone else in the village, they would be a normal couple who'd married while they were away visiting Evie's mother in Sussex.

'Come and sit,' Hettie urged them. 'I've baked a special cake to celebrate and we can have a drop of elderberry wine.'

Sitting around the table, with Ned by her side, Evie held Thea's gaze as her friend made a toast.

'To our dear Evie and Ned. May you have a very happy and long life together.' Thea raised her glass of ruby red wine. 'To Evie and Ned!'

The others followed, chorusing, 'To Evie and Ned!'

'Thank you,' Evie said, her eyes filling with tears. 'Your support means everything to us. I'm going to miss you all so much when I move out.'

'When do you think that might be?' Hettie asked, passing Evie a plate with a serving of cake that was plump with pieces of apple and fragrant with cinnamon.

'I don't know. It depends how soon we can find a place to

live. We know it might not be easy, with the village being so packed these days.'

'I could sleep on a camp bed in the dining room till you find somewhere, then Ned could stay here,' Flo suggested.

'Thank you, Flo, for the kind offer,' Evie said, giving her friend and roommate a grateful smile. 'But we can't let you do that. You need your sleep, the proper sleep that you get from lying on a comfortable mattress not on a cramped camp bed.'

'Evie's right, a camp bed's too uncomfortable for more than a night or two. Your back would soon be complaining,' Ned said. 'But thank you for the offer, Flo.'

'I'd be fine on the camp bed!' Flo insisted. 'Really I would.'

'You do hard, physical work in the garden all day, so need to keep fit and well rested,' Evie told her.

'It's generous of you, Flo,' Thea said. 'But Evie and Ned are right. We'll find another solution, don't worry. I only wish we had a spare bedroom, then Evie could stay here and Ned could move in too. Although starting a life together living with others probably isn't ideal. Best to have your own space and home.'

'Something will turn up,' Hettie reassured them. 'Mr and Mrs White will be in for a surprise when they find out you're married,' she said to Ned, who currently lodged with Great Plumstead Hall's head gardener and his wife in a cottage on the estate.

'I think they'll be delighted for us. Mr White thinks Evie's a smashing girl and he will say I'm a lucky man. He's right, I am.' Ned took hold of Evie's hand and kissed it. 'I'm a very lucky man and a happy one too.'

After their week away together in Sussex, followed by the two nights at the hotel in Suffolk, it felt odd to have to say goodbye to Ned a little while later. Evie walked out to the gate with him, hand in hand, to say their farewells in private and eek out their time together for a bit longer, making the most of every precious second.

'I wish we didn't have to go our separate ways,' Evie said. 'Me staying here and you going back to Gardener's Cottage.'

'So do I, but it won't be for long, I hope,' Ned said, his face shining in the moonlight. 'I'll miss you tonight.'

'I'll miss you, too. It's not the normal way to do things, saying goodnight and going to our separate homes now we're *married*.'

Ned's mouth curved with amusement. 'Nothing about our marriage is normal, is it? But I like that. It's good to do things in our own way. I won't ever regret it, Evie.'

Evie laughed. 'Like saying our promises in a bluebell wood? I'll never forget that.'

'I should hope not! I don't get down on my knees and declare my love to just anyone… only you, Evie.' He cupped her cheeks in the palms of his hands and then kissed her. Finally stepping back, Ned smiled at her. 'I'll go and see Lady Campbell-Gryce tomorrow and ask if there's anything available on the estate that we could rent.'

He pulled Evie into his arms and she rested her head against his chest for a moment before rocking back and looking up at him. 'We must make sure we spend time together every day. Just the two of us.'

'I promise we will.' Ned gently stroked her hair. 'I want to see my *wife* as often as I can.'

∽

Tired from travelling and needing to be up early for her shift at the hospital the next day, Evie was already in bed by the time Flo came up to the room they shared a little after half past nine. Once Flo had changed into her nightgown and climbed into her single bed, she lay on her side and turned to face Evie across the width of the rag rug separating their beds.

'It was lovely to celebrate with you and Ned tonight.' Flo's eyes reflected the light from the candle standing on the nightstand between their beds. 'You both look so happy. I'm glad you're taking this chance to be together.'

Evie smiled across at her friend. 'I love Ned very much and it feels right us being together. We have no need for the legal bit, although... we did have our own ceremony of sorts, in a bluebell wood close to my mother's house.'

'Is that when Ned gave you the ring?'

Evie nodded. 'He made a promise to me and I made one to him. It wasn't planned. Ned surprised me.' Evie paused as she recalled the special moment. 'It was as good as... no, actually it was *better* than a proper official wedding. It was just Ned and I together, making our commitment to each other, watched over by the towering beech trees.'

'It sounds perfect. So meaningful – and *very* romantic.' Flo reached her arm across the space and squeezed Evie's hand. 'I'm so happy for you both.'

'Thank you.' Evie squeezed her friend's hand back. 'My life is changing and, at some point, I'll be moving out of here to be with Ned. That's going to feel bittersweet. As much as I want to be with him, I'll miss living here at Rookery House with you all. It's such a wonderful home and you've all become like family to me.'

'I'll miss you, we all will,' Flo said wistfully. 'But you'll be with Ned and I think he's worth moving from Rookery House for. We'll still be here and you can visit any time.'

'I will, I promise you that. Rookery House and the people who live here will *always* be very special to me. But I'm not gone yet, and I plan to enjoy every moment I have left here.'

CHAPTER 6

With the last of today's Rural Pie Scheme pies delivered to the gardeners at Great Plumstead Hall, Prue slowed her pace, determined to enjoy every moment of the walk back to the village on such a glorious spring day. Heading down the long, tree-lined drive leading from the Hall, pushing the pram she'd borrowed from Gloria to transport the pies, Prue was surprised to spot a familiar figure emerge from the woods to her left. It was Lady Campbell-Gryce, with her dog trotting obediently at her heels.

'Good afternoon, Prue!' her Ladyship called, raising her hand.

'Good afternoon,' Prue returned the greeting. This was the first time she'd seen her friend since last week when her Ladyship had asked Prue to accompany her to York.

'I've been waiting for you,' Lady Campbell-Gryce said in a hushed voice as she drew near. 'I know you come along here every Monday with the pie delivery. Thought it best to make it look like a chance meeting. And I don't want to be overheard.' She glanced around her as she patted the head of her dog, who'd sat down obediently by his mistress. 'I've made the arrangements for York. We'll leave next Wednesday the twenty-eighth and return home on Monday the third of May. That will give us plenty of time to do what's needed and for you to spend time with Alice and explore the city. Is that all right with you?'

'Yes,' Prue confirmed. 'Now I know the dates I can arrange cover for my various shifts – that shouldn't be a problem.'

'Thank you!' Her Ladyship put her hand on Prue's arm. 'I appreciate you coming with me because I'm not sure I'd have the courage to follow the whole thing through on my own. I know there's no guarantee it will work, but I must try.' She let out a soft sigh. 'I thought it best if we don't appear to be leaving Great Plumstead together – I know how easily gossip can spread in the village. So although we'll get the same train, I'll sit in first class as usual to start with and then you can join me there once we're on our way. I'll buy the tickets so don't worry about that.'

'That's sounds like a good idea,' Prue agreed. 'If we look like we're going somewhere together it's bound to set tongues wagging.'

Her Ladyship nodded. 'It will be far better if we aren't the subject of gossips. I'll see you next Wednesday on the half past nine train?'

'I'll be there. And I really hope you can sort out the problem.'

'So do I, otherwise I'm not sure what to do.' Lady Campbell-Gryce raised her chin. 'But let's not go there. One step at a time and hopefully our trip will put a stop to it and bring Anthony to his senses. And now I must get on; I have a meeting at the hospital this afternoon. I'll see you next week and thank you again for your help.' After giving Prue a warm parting smile, Lady Campbell-Gryce headed off towards the

Hall looking as if she had merely stopped to chat about the weather and not about the details of a secret mission to catch her husband with his mistress, Prue thought.

As Prue continued her walk down the drive towards the village she was filled with a curious mix of feelings about the coming trip to York. There was both excitement and worry about the plan to catch his Lordship with his mistress – could they do it? It was rather like something out of a film at the pictures, with covert plans, undercover communications… and the future of her Ladyship's marriage, home and reputation hanging in the balance. Prue was already feeling the flutter of nerves in her stomach at the thought of what might happen when Anthony was confronted. Though on top of it all, she was also aware of a great joy at being able to see Alice while she was in York. That part of the trip was something Prue was looking forward to very much indeed.

CHAPTER 7

'If you don't mind me saying so, you've not been yourself these past couple of days,' Hettie said. 'Is something bothering you?'

Marianne glanced at her friend as they walked towards the village on their way to this afternoon's session of The Mother's Day Club at the village hall. Marianne was pushing Bea in the pram and the little girl was sitting up and looking out, while Emily skipped alongside pointing things out to her younger sister.

'I can't hide anything from you, can I? And you're right, there is something bothering me.' Marianne nodded her head towards the girls and lowered her voice, leaning closer towards Hettie so only she could hear what she had to say. 'Last Friday I had a phone call from Alex's sister, Marguerite.'

Hettie raised her eyebrows behind her round glasses. 'What did she want? Has she upset you?'

'Not intentionally on her part. She rang to say that she wants to come and visit. Meet the girls and get to know me better,' Marianne explained.

'Why now? She's not bothered before and wasn't at your wedding.'

'She's in the Wrens and has recently been posted to somewhere on the coast here in Norfolk. She would like to come when she has some time off – she couldn't say when though.'

'But it's worrying you. Do you think there might be another reason behind it?' Hettie probed. 'I remember very well what happened when her mother came.'

Marianne nodded, biting her bottom lip. Hettie had been there on that awful day and had swooped in to defend Marianne from her forceful, over-bearing mother-in-law.

'I don't know if Marguerite has another motive for wanting to see me but I can't help worrying that she has,' Marianne admitted. 'I've not heard anything from Alex's mother since we found out he was alive and a POW and therefore she had no chance of raising my children the way she wanted to. But it's always been like a dark cloud hanging over me that she'll try again. Or find some new way to interfere against my wishes. I expect I'll only be entirely free of the worry my children could be taken away when Alex is home and by my side again.'

'You poor thing.' Hettie shook her head. 'Would you like me to be there when Alex's sister visits, just in case?'

'Would you?'

'Of course I will. I'm not letting anyone upset you or these girls.' Hettie kept her voice low but Marianne could hear the passion in it.

'Thank you.' Marianne gave her friend a grateful smile. 'I don't know when it will be though.'

'That don't matter; just as soon as you find out let me know and I'll make sure I'm with you. Until then, try not to let it worry you,' Hettie advised. 'I know it's not always easy, but if it turns out fine then you'll have wasted all that precious time and energy worrying over nothing. It's a lesson I learned a long time ago and one worth following if you can.' Hettie waved her hand towards the girls. 'You've already got enough to keep your mind busy, without adding to it unnecessarily.'

Marianne managed a smile. 'You're right, Hettie. I'll try my best not to dwell on it. And I'm already reassured, knowing you'll be by my side. Thank you!'

'Anytime!' Hettie chuckled. 'Now I think there's been another delivery of holey socks from the aerodrome so I suppose it will be an afternoon of darning at The Mother's Day Club.'

'Darning – and chatting,' Marianne said more brightly. 'And laughing!' And that was just what she needed right now, she thought. Darning socks would keep her fingers busy while the good company, chatter and laughter from the other women would raise her spirits and help her do as Hettie advised and not spend time worrying about things that hadn't happened yet – and might never happen.

CHAPTER 8

Back at work as a Voluntary Aid Detachment Nurse at Great Plumstead Hall Hospital, Evie had been waiting for the right opportunity to speak to Matron Reed about her new situation. Now it was half past one and the nursing staff had just finished their meal, eating it together at the table in the nurses' sitting room as they always did. If Evie didn't ask to speak to Matron now, then the day may well pass by and it would seem odd – and perhaps a little bit suspicious – that she hadn't told her boss on her first day back at work.

'Matron, could I speak to you please?' Evie asked, hurrying to catch up as the older woman got up, pushed in her chair and headed for the door.

'Yes, what is it?' Matron asked tersely, her shrewd brown eyes questioning.

'Could we talk in your office, please?' Evie didn't want to tell Matron in front of her colleagues, though they would of course know soon enough. But if she was going to face a grilling, then she'd rather do so in the privacy of Matron's office.

'Very well,' Matron agreed. 'Although it will have to be quick, I have a meeting soon with the hospital's commandant and quartermaster.'

Evie followed Matron in to her office, closed the door behind them and stood waiting with her hands clasped behind her back while her boss settled herself down on her chair behind her desk.

'What is it you want to speak to me about?' Matron asked, fixing her steady gaze on Evie's face.

Evie was sure there was a hint of a smile at the corner of Matron's mouth, but she couldn't be certain – it might just be a touch of indigestion. It was best never to assume anything with Matron.

'I'm…' Evie hesitated, not wanting to tell a direct untruth to Matron. The woman was a hard task master to her staff but was always fair and straightforward. So, instead, Evie held out her left hand so that Matron could see the gold band on her finger. Her heart rate increased as she waited for Matron's reaction.

'Did you think I hadn't already noticed?' Matron said in her soft Scottish accent, her eyes twinkling with amusement. 'I spotted it at this morning's briefing before the start of your shift. I've been wondering when you were going to tell me. So you and Ned married while you were away in Sussex – did you get a special licence?'

Evie nodded. She'd been ready for people to ask about them needing a special licence. Having one meant there was no need for the usual reading of banns in a church over several weeks before a wedding. Getting a special licence was a common occurrence these days – with so many people's lives being ruled by the armed forces and the war effort in general, time was often severely limited. So that part of her and Ned's story was unlikely to cause raised eyebrows.

'We made our vows to each other,' Evie said truthfully. 'It was lovely.'

Matron's face broke into a wide, beaming smile. She leapt to her feet, came round to the front of her desk and took both of Evie's hands in hers. 'I'm delighted for you both, I truly am. I wish you many happy years together.'

'Thank you, Matron.' Evie smiled as relief flooded through her. She was amazed to see such effervescent joy from the older woman who tended to be far quicker to criticise than praise.

'You make a fine couple and are extremely well suited. What are your plans?'

'Plans? Evie asked.

'Well *traditionally* nurses leave their jobs when they marry… I'll be sorry to lose you. You're an excellent nurse, Nurse Jones, or rather I should say now, Nurse Blythe.'

'But I don't want to leave!' Evie burst out, tears smarting her eyes. She'd been so wrapped up in finding a way to be with Ned that she hadn't considered one consequence might be losing the job she loved. How could she have been so foolish? She'd never known a colleague who'd left because they'd got married… though she must have vaguely known that was what used to happen. Now, though, surely the demands of wartime meant such traditions were obsolete.

Evie blinked the tears away and looked Matron in the eye. 'I *promise* you that being married won't stop me from being a good nurse. I can assure you, Matron, that my standards will remain at the highest level. Please let me stay.'

Matron nodded. 'I certainly have no objection to you carrying on working here if you're willing. However, I'll have to check with Lady Campbell-Gryce since she's our commandant. I will ask her at this afternoon's meeting. She will have the final say in the matter.' Matron pursed her lips thoughtfully. 'Since your role is a voluntary one – and as you are still willing to keep on volunteering – then I don't see why it should be a problem.'

'Thank you!' Evie said. 'Being Ned's wife won't stop me doing my job to the best of my abilities.'

'I'm sure it won't,' Matron agreed. 'Where are you living now?'

'I'm at Rookery House and Ned's still lodging with Mr and Mrs White at Gardener's Cottage. We're hoping we can find somewhere together soon. Ned's going to have a word with Lady Campbell-Gryce, see if there's anything available on the estate.'

'I hope something can be found for you together. Starting married life living apart isn't ideal.' Matron glanced at her watch. 'I must get ready for the meeting. Congratulations again, Nurse Blythe. I'm happy for you both. It must have been that mistletoe hanging in the Hall last Christmas working it's magic.' She chuckled, then patted Evie's shoulder. 'And don't worry, I will raise your request to keep working and let you know as soon as a decision has been made. Now – we both have work to do, Nurse Blythe.'

Leaving Matron's office, Evie recalled how Matron had encouraged her and Ned to make use of the bunch of mistletoe hanging in the hallway last Christmas Day. Matron had clearly always been on their side and Evie hoped her support would be enough to prevent Evie losing the job she loved.

~

'I knew there was something different about you!' Hazel, Evie's friend and fellow nurse, declared after throwing her arms around Evie. 'You are positively glowing with married bliss!'

Evie laughed as Hazel released her and she returned to her work, cutting up another length of lint to go in the metal canister to be sterilised before it could be used for dressing wounds. 'I'm very happy, that's why. I love Ned and he loves me.'

'I think it's so romantic what you've done,' Hazel said dreamily, returning to her seat and rolling up a length of bandage. 'Off you go on leave and come back a married couple, no fuss, no worrying about wedding dresses or that there's no icing for a cake.'

'It was certainly different to most traditional weddings but then it's wartime and needs must as they say,' Evie said, thinking of the beautiful bluebell wood where they had made their promises to each other.

'Do you…?' Hazel began but halted as the door to the storeroom where they were working opened and Lady Campbell-Gryce walked in.

'Good afternoon, Nurse Robertson and,' she paused, smiling at Evie, 'Nurse Blythe!'

Evie and Hazel quickly stood up, both returning her greeting.

'I hear congratulations are in order. I'm so pleased for you and Ned. Matron tells me that you've volunteered to stay on nursing for us, for which I am most grateful. We would hate to lose you.'

'Thank you. I'm delighted to be able to stay on. My work means a lot to me,' Evie said. She felt the weight that had settled on her shoulders earlier vanish with the good news.

'I saw Ned while I was taking a stroll out in the garden after my meeting and he asked about some accommodation for you both together on the estate,' her Ladyship said. 'I'll see what I can do and let you know as soon as I can – you don't want to start your married life living apart for very long. Now I must get on, lots to organise.'

After Lady Campbell-Gryce had gone, they sat down again. Evie leaned back in her chair, letting out a soft sigh.

'Thank goodness she said I can stay on. I honestly don't know what I'd have done if they'd made me leave my job.'

'I'm glad you're not going,' Hazel said, giving Evie a warm smile. 'I'd have missed you so much. Now you just need to find somewhere to live with Ned and then you'll be all settled, Nurse Blythe!' Hazel emphasised Evie's new surname. 'I'm bound to get it wrong sometimes and call you Nurse Jones for a bit. But I'll do my best to remember.'

'Don't worry,' Evie reassured her friend. 'We have rather sprung it on everyone. I'm still getting used to it myself!'

CHAPTER 9

It was breakfast time at Rookery House and everyone was settled around the kitchen table eating their bowls of porridge, stewed apple and honey except for Evie, who'd left earlier for her shift at the hospital.

'We need to get another lot of peas sown this morning, some dwarf beans and beetroot...' Thea said, writing them down on a list. 'Anything else?'

'What about carrots and spinach?' Flo asked from her seat opposite.

'Yes, those too.' Thea added them to the list, then scooped up another spoonful of her porridge.

'And I would suggest we do more lettuce,' Flo added, 'if we have time.'

'Sounds like you've got a busy day ahead,' Marianne said as she prepared another small mouthful of porridge for Bea who was sitting happily on her lap.

'Yes indeed!' Thea agreed. 'It's that time of year. Every day is a busy day now.'

'Can we help, when we get home from school?' George asked.

'We'll save the marrows for you, Betty, Emily and Bea to plant, how's that?' Thea suggested, smiling at the little boy.

George's eyes shone. 'Yes please, Auntie Thea!'

'We could stay at home all day helping instead of going to school,' Betty suggested, giving Thea a persuasive look.

'No, you can't go missing school,' Hettie said, reaching over and putting her hand on Betty's shoulder. 'Though it's a kind offer.'

'It is, and thank you,' Thea agreed. 'We'll save the marrows for when you get home, all right?'

'Okay, Auntie Thea.' Betty seemed content and began scraping her bowl for the last scraps of creamy porridge.

Hettie had just finished her own breakfast when the telephone started to ring in the hall, causing everyone to pause.

Thea began to get up to answer it, but Hettie waved her friend to sit down again. 'I'll go,' she said, standing up.

Making her way into the hall, Hettie wondered who might be telephoning at this time of day. Perhaps it was a Land Girl in need of assistance.

Picking up the receiver Hettie said, 'Rookery House.'

'Hettie, it's me,' a woman's voice came down the line.

'Nancy, is everything all right?' Hettie asked, recognising the young woman's distinctive East End accent. Nancy had been working for Thea here in the garden since last March.

'No, it ain't!' Nancy replied, wearily. 'I've been up more than 'alf the night with Joan – she's got a poorly tummy There's no going to school for 'er today, I'm afraid. Can you tell Thea I'm ever so sorry, but I've got to stay at 'ome to look after Joan?'

'Of course I will. I hope Joan soon feels better,' Hettie said.

'Thanks, Hettie. I'll be back to work as soon as I can. I…' Nancy paused and Hettie could hear a child's voice calling for her mother in the background. 'I've got to go,' Nancy added hurriedly and disconnected the call.

Hettie put the receiver down, thinking things must be fraught at Prue's house this morning, where Nancy and her two daughters, Joan and Marie, had lived since they'd been evacuated from London in 1940 after losing their home in the Blitz. Naturally Nancy had to put looking after her unwell child first but it did mean she'd be unable to come to work today.

It was a problem faced by all working mothers unless they had someone else who could look after their child for them. When Nancy had first come to work in the gardens her occasional need to take time off to care for her children when they were unwell had been a problem. Nancy had felt awful about letting Thea down because the work still needed doing and her not being there meant extra for everyone else. Thankfully, for both Nancy and Thea, they now had a back-up solution for days like this, someone who'd volunteered to step in and help when needed – and that was Ted.

The door from the kitchen opened and Thea came into the hall.

'Who was that?'

'Nancy,' Hettie said. 'Joan's ill and needs her mum to stay at home with her. Nancy said to say she's sorry and will be back as soon as she can.'

'Poor Joan,' Thea replied. 'What's the matter with her?'

'A stomach upset.'

'It will take her a few days to get over that.' Thea considered for a moment. 'We're getting busy in the garden with spring here. I think we'd better see if Ted can come and help. I'll go and ask him.'

'You don't need to do that. I can go,' Hettie offered. Like most homes in the village, there was no telephone at Ted's house so they couldn't simply ring.

Thea put a hand on Hettie's shoulder. 'Thanks, I appreciate that.'

'I always like a trip back to my old home and it's a nice day for a bike ride,' Hettie said. 'I'll go as soon as we've got breakfast over and the children off to school.'

~

Arriving at Ivy Cottage later that morning, Hettie felt a tug of homecoming, seeing the place where she'd once lived. She'd been born and had spent her childhood here with her parents, her brothers Sidney and Albert, and her sister Ada, until she'd left home to go and work at Great Plumstead Hall at the age of fourteen. Although it was many years since she or any of her family had lived here, Ivy Cottage was still deeply ingrained in her life, rather like one of the rings inside a tree trunk. Now it was home to Ted and his sister Hilda.

After leaning her bicycle against the wall of the cottage she knocked on the front door, then stepped back to admire the garden, which under Ted's care was planted out with vegetable beds and fruit bushes. Ted had been born in Great Plumstead and been best friends with Hettie's brothers growing up, but he'd spent most of his life working as a gardener and ended up as head gardener at the Hall where he'd worked in Suffolk. Hettie had only met Ted again once he'd returned here to enjoy his retirement.

'Hettie!'

She turned at the sound of her name to see Ted coming around the corner of the cottage. 'I thought I heard a knock,' he said.

'Hello Ted.' She gave him a warm smile which he returned.

'If you've come to see Hilda, then I'm afraid you're out of luck, she's gone into Wykeham.'

'It's you I've come to see,' Hettie told him.

'Me!' He gave her another broad smile. 'How can I help you?'

'It's not me you can help, but Thea. One of Nancy's girls is poorly so she's staying off work today to look after her…' Hettie began.

'Would Thea like me to fill in for Nancy for a day or so or however long it is until she's back?'

'Yes please, if you can, Thea would really appreciate it. With spring here it's a busy time of year in the garden as you know.' Hettie waved her hand towards one of Ted's vegetable beds where there were green shoots peeping through the soil. 'But you're probably busy enough here and don't have time to come and help in Rookery House's garden.'

'I can easily catch up with anything I need to do here,' Ted reassured her. 'What Thea does is on a much bigger scale and if she gets behind it's harder to catch up as there's so much to do. I've told her I'm happy to help and I meant it,' he reassured Hettie.

'Thank you. I'll make sure you have a good filling meal in the day to keep you going, help keep your energy up.'

'I will look forward to it. If you'll give me five minutes to get myself ready, then we can bicycle back to Rookery House together if you want.'

'That would be lovely. I'll wait here for you.'

A short while later they were cycling side by side along one of the village's quiet country lanes, heading for Rookery House.

'I had a letter from your Sidney yesterday,' Ted said. 'We

write to each other regularly now. It's been good to be in touch with him again after all these years.'

'You two always were as thick as thieves,' Hettie remarked, throwing Ted a grin. 'And I remember the two of you getting up to mischief, climbing trees and learning to swim in the river.' She had been delighted to be able to play a part in reuniting, via letter, the two boyhood friends. Sidney was now living in Canada, but she'd known how much her brother had liked Ted, the pair of them being similar in age, starting and finishing school at the same time. It was only them both moving to different places that had led to their friendship stalling as distance and busy working lives got in the way.

Ted laughed. 'We did indeed. I remember we never could persuade you to learn to swim.'

'That's because I didn't want to drown!' Hettie retorted. 'The pair of you seemed to spend more time under the water than on top of it.'

'We held our breath and watched the fishes swimming about. It's another world down there. The offer's still there if you'd like to learn now.'

Hettie chuckled. 'I'm well past learning to swim in a cold river. I'll stick to dry land, thank you very much.'

'Fair enough and a wise decision, I'm sure. I'm not sure I'd want to get in these days,' Ted admitted. 'I'd catch a cold I'm sure.'

'Best you stick to growing things, then. It's warmer – and safer.'

And she would hate any harm to come to Ted, she thought silently. They'd become good friends since he'd moved back here and she'd grown rather fond of him.

'*The Mask of Zorro* was just what we needed,' Flo said as she spread butter on a slice of bread to go with her bowl of soup. 'Whisked us away from wartime England to southern California. Marge and Elspeth loved it so much last night they said they might go and see it again.'

Hettie ladled out a bowl of soup and passed it to Ted, who after a morning's work alongside Thea and Flo in the garden, had come into the kitchen at Rookery House to join the midday meal.

'Thank you.' Ted gave Hettie a nod as he took the bowl from her. 'What did they like about it so much?' he asked, directing his question at Flo.

'Elspeth thought Tyrone Power was very dashing! He played the lead role of Zorro.' Flo dipped her spoon into her soup. 'And it was an exciting and glamorous adventure.'

'And very different to life as a Waaf, I'm sure,' Thea said.

'I'm glad you, Elspeth and Marge are friends and go out and have fun together,' Hettie said. 'With Evie now married and moving out soon it's important for you to have the company of people your own age and to get out of the house and enjoy yourself.'

'I suppose it's unusual for Land Girls and Waafs to be friends as they don't tend to meet often, doing very different jobs,' Flo said. 'If Marge and Elspeth hadn't come to stay here last year, we probably would never have met, even though they live on RAF Great Plumstead aerodrome.'

'We enjoyed having them stay with us,' Thea said. 'They still feel like part of our Rookery House family. I love it that they come back and see us so often.'

'I can't actually remember the last time I went to the pictures,' Hettie said, dipping her spoon into her soup. 'I was too busy when I was Cook at the Hall and I haven't been since I moved here.'

'Same with me,' Ted agreed. 'I haven't been to the pictures for years. Maybe we should go, Hettie. And see what this *Mask of Zorro* is all about.'

Hettie considered for a moment. 'Yes, why not? Let's all go to the pictures in Wykeham. Who wants to come besides me and Ted?'

'Oh what a shame we can't join you!' Flo said, giving Thea a knowing look. 'We'll be doing extra shifts in the greenhouse, won't we Thea?'

Thea returned Flo's look. 'Yes, we do have a lot on and we can always take a trip to the pictures once Nancy's back and our planting out is in hand. Springtime is so busy.'

'Looks like it's just the two of you, then,' said Flo. 'I'm sure you'll have a lovely time together.'

'How about on Saturday afternoon?' Ted suggested. 'Will *The Mask of Zorro* still be on then?'

'I don't know,' Hettie said. 'But if it isn't, then it doesn't matter. The important thing is we'll be going to the pictures to see a film, something we both haven't done in a very long time. It will be fun.'

CHAPTER 10

'I'm going to need someone to cover for me next Wednesday,' Prue said, glancing across the cab of the WVS canteen at her sister, who was driving. 'Do you think one of the others will step in and do my shift for me?'

'I'm sure someone will; you've often helped out when someone else needed their shift covered.' Thea turned her head to look at Prue briefly, a questioning look on her face. 'What are you doing next Wednesday instead?'

'I'm going to York for a few days,' Prue said. 'I want to see Alice. She doesn't get much time off to come home, so I've decided that I shall go to see her.'

'She'll be pleased to see you.' Thea threw Prue a smile. 'What made you decide to go next week?'

As much as she'd like to, Prue couldn't tell her sister that she was going on a secret mission with Lady Campbell-Gryce. Her Ladyship trusted Prue and she couldn't betray that trust, not even to Thea.

'It's rather a spur of the moment decision,' Prue said. 'I miss Alice so much and I'm worried about her with next week being the first anniversary of Victor's death. Alice might find it hard. It's bound to bring back a lot of memories for her. Despite how Victor was, Alice did love him.'

'She's got a kind heart. I remember how stunned and upset she was at his funeral,' Thea recalled. 'It was a terrible shock to her and she didn't know the half of it, either.'

'And I hope she never will!' Prue had never told any of her children the truth about where Victor was when he'd been killed. They didn't know that their father had had a mistress, who, Prue later found out, he was supposedly engaged to. She'd made the decision to keep Victor's deceitful behaviour from them, thinking it would only cause more harm than good. Each of them had seen and been on the receiving end of their father's unpleasant behaviour at one time or another and had their own opinions of him. There was no need to add to it and burden them further. Besides, Victor having a mistress wasn't about anyone else – it was between Victor and Prue and his breaking of his marriage vows to her.

'My plan is to spend some time in York together with Alice. RAF Elvington, where she's stationed, isn't too far from there and it's much easier for her to meet me in York than come all the way home to Great Plumstead,' Prue told Thea.

Thea changed gear, slowing the canteen as they approached their first visit of the day, one of their regular stops. 'I'm sure you'll have a good time. I look forward to hearing about it when you're back.' Thea glanced at Prue. 'It will do you good to have a holiday too. You're always busy and never seem to stop for a rest. At least by taking yourself off to York, you can have a break from helping other people for once!' Thea turned the canteen in through the gateway leading to the searchlight battery station.

Prue smiled inwardly at the irony of her sister's words; it was precisely because she'd been asked to help someone that she was going to York! Although at least accompanying Lady Campbell-Gryce gave Prue the wonderful bonus of being able to see Alice.

'Enough talk of holidays.' Thea switched off the engine and gave Prue a cheeky look. 'We've work to do first and plenty of eager customers outside.' She nodded to where the soldiers were heading their way, ready to buy some food or hot drinks, or stock up on any of the small items stocked by the canteen.

'What a shame my holiday doesn't start till next week!' Prue retorted with a laugh. 'Let's get on with it!'

CHAPTER 11

It was a week today, Evie thought, since she and Ned had made their vows to each other amongst a sea of bluebells and underneath a canopy of towering beech trees. After a brief honeymoon, their first week back at work as a married couple had been busy for them both.

With spring bursting forth, Ned had been working hard in the Hall's large, walled kitchen garden and Evie's long shifts gave her little time to spare. She'd done her best to see him as often as she could, squeezing in some time together by popping out to be with him in the garden during her breaks, but it was never enough.

Ned waited for Evie each evening and, after she'd finished her shift, accompanied her back to Rookery House, bicycling along beside her and talking of his day before returning to his lodgings for the night. Evie did her best to be grateful for their fragments of time together, but she hoped more suitable arrangements for a married couple could be found – and the sooner the better.

This afternoon, Evie and Ned were meeting Lady

Campbell-Gryce outside in the courtyard at the back of the Hall. She'd sent a message to each of them, asking them to meet her here at two o'clock.

'Do you think her Ladyship has found somewhere for us to live?' Evie asked Ned as they waited. 'She must have, otherwise why would she ask us to meet her here. What do you think, Ned? Should we get our hopes up?'

'She could just have sent a message if it was to say no.' Ned put his arm around Evie's waist and pulled her close to him. 'We'll soon find out one way or the other. If she can't help us, well then we'll just keep looking. Something will turn up for us, Evie. We will be able to live together, even if it takes a bit longer.'

Evie glanced at the watch pinned to the front of her blue nurse's uniform. 'It's gone two o'clock, nearly five past. Do you think she's forgotten?'

'Here she comes now.' Ned turned towards the wooden gate leading from the walled garden, which Lady Campbell-Gryce had just opened and stepped through. She closed the gate behind her and gave them a winning smile as she strode towards them.

'Good afternoon, Evie, Ned. I've just been looking over the plans for the kitchen garden with Mr White. I must say everything's looking good for another year's productive growing. We'll be able to keep our patients well fed,' she said. 'Now, I'm sure you're anxious to know if I've found somewhere for you to live. Well, as I suspected, we have no empty cottages available on the estate at present.' Evie's heart sank. 'But there is another possibility, rather different from a cottage but it could work well for you both and importantly would mean you could live together instead of one of you at Gardener's Cottage and the other at Rookery House. Nice places though they both might be. So follow me and see what I've come up with.'

Without waiting for a response, her Ladyship turned on her heels and marched across to the far side of the wide, cobbled courtyard towards the old stables where Evie and the other nurses parked their bicycles.

Following behind, Evie glanced at Ned who gave her a quizzical look in return, looking as unsure about what Lady Campbell-Gryce had in mind as Evie.

Her Ladyship halted by the far end of the stable block, took a key out of her jacket pocket and used it to unlock a solid wooden door facing into the courtyard. She pushed it open to reveal a hallway with a flight of stairs going up. There was a row of pegs on the wall for outdoor clothing and plenty of room for boots and shoes underneath. An inner door led off to the right.

Stepping into the hallway, Lady Campbell-Gryce put her hand on the inner door handle before turning to face them. 'Now I want you to use your imaginations, picture how these old grooms' rooms *could* look,' she said, her tone upbeat. 'Don't dwell on how things appear right now. Look beyond the dust and cobwebs because I think after a jolly good clean, a lick of fresh paint and with some furniture this place could make a lovely home for you both. A bonus is it would be just a few yards from where you both work. Follow me.'

As she stepped in through the outside doorway, Evie realised that she'd never considered what lay beyond the heavy wooden door, even though she'd passed it every day since she'd come to work here. The door had always been closed and the small windows looking out to the courtyard – one beside the door and a row on the upper floor above the stables – were always dark.

'In here to the right is the kitchen,' Lady Campbell-Gryce

said as Evie and Ned followed her into the room. 'It's basic as the grooms used to eat in the servants' hall in the house, but it was somewhere they could make a hot drink and some simple food if they wanted.'

Evie looked around the room which was indeed basic. It had a sink below a window which looked out in the direction of the kitchen garden, a black iron stove and some wooden shelving. The floor was grey with dust, their footprints stirring it sufficiently to show the red tiles underneath which, Evie noticed, were similar to the ones on the kitchen floor at Rookery House.

'It obviously needs a table, chairs and a dresser or cupboard for storing your crockery and things,' her Ladyship said, waving her hand around. 'And through there,' she pointed to another door leading off the kitchen, 'is a scullery which leads through to a lavatory.' She led them through to the scullery where there was another sink and a copper for heating water. Evie noticed a tin bath hanging on the wall.

'There's no proper bathroom I'm afraid. I suppose you could always use one of the bathrooms at the hospital for a bath,' her Ladyship suggested.

'I'm used to using a tin bath at Gardener's Cottage,' Ned said.

Her Ladyship nodded. 'Of course. Now come upstairs and see the bedrooms.' She led the way out of the kitchen and up the flight of stairs.

As Evie climbed the stairs behind Lady Campbell-Gryce and Ned, she wondered if these rooms, that had once housed the Hall's grooms, could be a home for her and Ned? They weren't like a cottage, but they had all the necessities for living that they'd need, including the tin bath.

At the top of the stairs there was a long corridor running the length of the block, with three doors leading off it on the left, and two windows on the right-hand wall which looked out over the cobbled yard to the back of the Hall and the servants' entrance. 'There are three bedrooms up here. You could use one for a sitting room,' Lady Campbell-Gryce suggested. She opened the nearest door and stepped aside for them to look in.

Evie saw that the room was as dusty and cobwebby as those on the ground floor but otherwise in perfectly good order. She stepped inside and walked over to the window, which was grimy with dirt but not bad enough to completely obscure the view into the walled kitchen garden, which would grow even lovelier as spring progressed into summer.

'What do you think?' Lady Campbell-Gryce asked. 'It would be lovely to have these rooms used again and made into your home.'

Evie glanced at Ned and he gave a nod, his eyes meeting hers.

'We'd love to take it!' Evie walked across the room and held out her hand to her Ladyship. 'Thank you very much. We can soon clean it up and make it into our first home together. It will be ideal.'

Lady Campbell-Gryce smiled broadly as she shook Evie's hand and then Ned's. 'Excellent. I'm delighted for you both. There's plenty of furniture in the Hall's attics that could be of use to you, so once you've got the rooms cleaned up and you know what you need, please ask my housekeeper Mrs Kilburn to take you up there so you can choose some things.'

'Thank you, that's so kind of you,' Evie said.

'I'll leave you both to have a good look around then you can decide what needs doing. You'll need this.' Her Ladyship held out the key to Evie.

Evie took the large key and wrapped her fingers around it as it lay in the palm of her hand. It felt so heavy, so important

– and it was. It was the key to the beginning of their proper married life together.

'I wish you both much happiness here,' Lady Campbell-Gryce said. 'I look forward to seeing how you turn these rooms into your new home.'

Left alone after her Ladyship had gone, Evie threw herself into Ned's arms. 'I never expected this! It's perfect for us, even if it's full of dust and cobwebs right now. It's nothing some hard work scrubbing and cleaning won't fix. I've got plenty of experience scrubbing floors and washing down walls and furniture in the hospital, so that won't be a problem. I can't wait to get it ready and move in.'

'We'll soon make this place the way we want it,' Ned said, planting a kiss on her lips. 'This will be our first home together. We'll be very happy here, Evie.'

∼

That evening, after Evie had arrived home at Rookery House and eaten the meal that had been left keeping warm for her, she joined the others in the sitting room. Hettie was knitting and Marianne was doing some hand sewing, while Flo and Thea were both reading. The children were all in bed.

'Hello, Evie,' Thea said, looking up from her book, 'have you had a good day?'

'I have.' Evie sat down on the sofa next to Flo, who patted her arm. 'I have some news. Ned and I have found somewhere to live!'

'Where?' Hettie asked, her blue eyes widening behind her round glasses.

'In the old grooms' quarters at the Hall's stables,' Evie told them, looking around at her friends who were all listening intently. 'Lady Campbell-Gryce showed Ned and I around this afternoon and offered them to us and we accepted!'

'That's such good news,' Thea said. 'Although we will miss you, of course. When are you moving?'

'I should think those rooms need a good clean,' Hettie said, her fingers working fast as she knitted. 'They haven't been lived in for quite a while.'

'They do need work,' Evie agreed. 'There's an awful lot of dust and plenty of cobwebs to be got rid of first. It will take us a while before we can move in.'

'I'll help you with the cleaning,' Flo offered.

'And so will we,' Thea said, glancing at Hettie who nodded her agreement.

'What about curtains?' Marianne asked. 'Do you need some? I could make them for you.'

Evie thought for a moment, trying to picture if there were any at the windows, but couldn't remember for sure. And even if there were, they would probably be moth-eaten. 'Thank you, Marianne, I accept your kind offer and all of your offers of help.'

Evie got up and gave each of her friends a hug. 'Thank you all,' she said, 'for this and everything.'

When she'd sat down again, Hettie suggested, 'I dare say there's some material up in the Hall's attics you could use for making curtains. I know her Ladyship donated a lot of material to The Mother's Day Club for making garments for the clothing depot, but Ada told me there's still plenty left in the attics.'

'Lady Campbell-Gryce said I should speak to Ada about looking in the attics for furniture, saying we should take what we need,' Evie said. Ada was Hettie's sister and had lived here at Rookery House for a while before getting the job as housekeeper at the Hall, so Evie knew her quite well.

'Ada will soon sort you out,' Hettie said. 'She had a good tidy up of the attics when she was finding material for her Ladyship, so she knows what's up there.'

'Let us know when you're starting the cleaning and we can come along and help,' Thea said.

'Thank you so much, I will. I'm going to have to fit it in around my shifts at the hospital.'

'Then you'll be a long while getting it done…' Flo warned. 'You only get one day off a week and one weekend every month.'

'In that case,' said Thea, 'we'll make a start on Sunday.'

'But that's your day off from work,' Evie said. 'You don't want to spend it cleaning.'

'We want to help you and Ned,' Hettie said firmly. 'That's what friends do. We three will be there on Sunday afternoon and make a start, and no arguing!'

CHAPTER 12

'Is here all right for you, Hettie?' Ted asked, stopping halfway down the steps inside the dimly lit auditorium of the Regal Picture House in Wykeham on Saturday afternoon.

'It will do just fine.' Hettie took off her coat and draped it over the neighbouring empty seat and settled herself down on the second seat in, leaving the seat by the aisle for Ted. 'It's been far too long since I last came here. I'm glad you suggested it.'

The lights dimmed further and the curtains swished open, revealing the screen which became peppered with black and white circles for a few moments as the Pathé Film news reel began to play, showing a report about the war.

Hettie found herself transfixed by the images she saw playing out before her. They showed the reality of how the war was faring in far-off lands, with soldiers on the move in a war zone, dressed in uniform, guns poised as they marched. It was so much more immediate and telling than the many words she'd read in newspaper reports, and it brought the harsh nature of the war home in a far more powerful way. As the scene changed to one of wounded soldiers after a battle, and even some dead bodies, Hettie let out a gasp, putting a hand to her mouth. She felt Ted take hold of her left hand, giving it a gentle squeeze, and she kept hold of his, grateful for his support. Hettie and Ted were still holding hands when the news reel ended and there was a pause before the film started.

'That was more shocking than reading about what's going on in the newspaper,' Hettie said in a low voice, aware of other people sitting not far off. 'Brings it home to you, doesn't it?'

'The saying *a picture is worth a thousand words* is so true,' Ted said. 'We don't know the half of it just reading the newspaper and listening to the wireless. Seeing it with your own eyes puts a whole new perspective on it. But we mustn't let it dampen our enjoyment of this afternoon too much.'

'I'm ready to watch Zorro's story even more now.' Hettie gave Ted's hand another squeeze before letting it go as the introductory credits of the film began to play out on the screen and rousing music filled the auditorium. She settled back further into her seat and let herself be carried away.

By the time the final credits began to roll, Hettie felt as if she'd been whisked off from the picture house in Wykeham and was now having to return to reality with a bump. It had been a wonderful film. It made her laugh, gasp, cheer and get behind the heroics of Zorro and his leading lady as they faced their challenges.

'What did you think?' Ted asked as the lights came on and the other filmgoers started to leave.

'Marvellous!' Hettie beamed at him. 'I feel like I've been away on a short holiday! Did you like it?'

'I did, very much,' Ted agreed. 'I…'

'Hettie, Ted!' A voice called to them from the other side of the auditorium and Hettie looked round to see the two Waafs, Elspeth and Marge, waving at them, before making their way along a row of seats towards them.

'You came back to see the film again,' Hettie said. 'Flo said you were keen on it.'

'We are! That Tyrone Power...' Elspeth put her hand on the front of her blue WAAF tunic, over her heart. 'I could watch him all day long.'

'That was the final showing of Zorro before a new film starts tonight,' Marge said. 'We had to take our last chance to see it while we could. Did you both enjoy it?'

'We did. It's the first time we've been to the pictures for years. I'd like to come again soon,' Hettie said. 'I'd forgotten what an adventure it is.'

'There you go Ted, if you want a companion to come to the pictures with again, then Hettie's willing,' Elspeth said before giving Hettie a knowing look.

Hettie raised her eyebrows at the young woman, who'd met Ted last year at Rookery House and had noticed then that he seemed rather taken with Hettie.

'I was thinking it would be nice to go and have a cuppa in the tea shop if anyone would like to come with me,' Ted suggested.

'That would be lovely, thank you Ted,' Hettie agreed.

'We can't I'm afraid – we've got to get back to the aerodrome,' Marge said. 'We only managed to get here this afternoon by swapping duties, so we mustn't be late back. Thank you for the offer though.'

'Another time,' Elspeth said. 'We'd better get going, Marge. Good to see you both.'

After a quick farewell the pair of them hurried off.

'I'm glad we're not in such a hurry,' Hettie said, putting her coat on. 'Those young women live their lives at such a fast pace, they make the most of what spare time they have.'

'I suppose much of their life is ruled by the RAF so no wonder they enjoy their time off,' Ted said as they walked out of the picture house. 'Now where would you like to go, the tea shop on the corner of market square or the one opposite the church?'

'Gracie's, on the corner of market square. Their scones are always good,' Hettie said.

Ted chuckled. 'That's praise indeed coming from the former cook of Great Plumstead Hall.' He offered her his arm and Hettie put her hand through it and together they headed for the tea shop, their afternoon outing not over yet.

CHAPTER 13

Evie was taking her afternoon break and headed across the cobbled courtyard to see how things were progressing in the old grooms' rooms. She could see Flo was hard at work inside the kitchen, washing grime from the windowpanes. Flo spotted her approaching and waved. Evie waved back, grateful that her friend had given up her free time to come and help.

'Hello!' Evie called as she went in the front door into the hallway with its stairs leading to the upper floor.

'Evie! Come and see what we're doing!' Betty's voice bubbled with excitement as she appeared in the kitchen doorway. She grabbed hold of Evie's hand and tugged her inside.

Gone was the fusty smell of layers of dust. Now the air had the fresh, clean scent of hot soapy water which was being used to wash windows and clean floors. Ned, with George beside him, was down on his hands and knees, scouring the tiles with scrubbing brushes.

'We're cleaning all the dirt off the floor and there's a lot!' Betty picked up the scrubbing brush she'd abandoned when she heard Evie arriving and knelt on the hard surface. 'Watch!' She dipped her brush in a nearby bucket of soapy water and scrubbed at a patch of dirty grey floor, scrubbing at it furiously until she'd revealed the bright, orangey-red tile underneath. 'That's better, isn't it Evie?' she said, through deep breaths.

'Wonderful, Betty!' Evie clapped. 'But don't exhaust yourself!' The little girl smiled sheepishly.

Ned and George had both stopped to watch, leaning back on their heels.

'It's much improved without the layers of dirt on it!' Ned said. Evie noticed his face was smudged comically with dust. 'It's coming up beautifully, better even than I'd hoped.' He gestured at the large patch of floor they'd cleaned, where the warm colour of the tiles was catching the light streaming in from the windows, already transforming the room from a long unused space into a homely and attractive kitchen.

'You're all doing a wonderful job.' Evie gave them an appreciative smile.

'And Flo's cleaning the windows,' George piped up.

Evie turned to her friend. 'They look so much better! Thank you, Flo.'

'It will be smashing in here when it's all done and when you've got furniture and your things moved in. It will make a cosy home for sure,' Flo said. 'Thea, Hettie and Marianne are busy too. They're working their own magic upstairs.'

'I'll pop up and see them. I'm meeting Ada in the Hall at half past two.' Evie glanced at her watch pinned to the front of her blue uniform dress and saw she had just over ten minutes until she was due to meet Hettie's sister. 'She's taking me up to the attics to look for some suitable furniture, curtains and things.'

Leaving them to carry on with their cleaning, Evie went

out of the kitchen and up the flight of stairs. She met Marianne, carrying Bea and with Emily following on behind, coming along the corridor towards her.

'Hello,' Marianne greeted her. 'I'm taking these two back to Rookery House. It's for the best.' She gave a rueful smile. 'A one-year-old and a three-year-old are more likely to get in the way here than help, but I've taken measurements for all the windows and can alter the curtains you choose to fit them.'

'Thanks, I'm sure Ada and I will find some suitable ones.'

'We'll see you later.' Marianne headed off down the stairs, going slowly so that Emily could walk safely behind her.

'We're in here, Evie!' Hettie's voice called from a room at the far end of the corridor.

Evie walked on and stopped in the open doorway where she was met once again by the fresh, clean smell of her friends' hard work. Hettie and Thea were washing down the walls with more hot, soapy water. She thought that it must have been a long time since this place had seen so much of the stuff and the elbow grease that goes with it. If ever, perhaps, as the grooms who'd lived here might not have been very house proud!

'Ned cleaned all the cobwebs and dead flies away,' Thea said. 'But there's still a layer of dust on the walls that needs coming off.' She carried on washing the wall, using a broom with a wet soapy cloth around it to reach the highest parts.

'I've been trying to remember how long it's been since there were any grooms living here,' Hettie said. 'So many of them didn't come home from the Great War and then the next generation of Campbell-Gryces were more interested in driving cars than riding horses. No wonder the place has got so mucky.'

'It's looking so much better already,' Evie said. 'I feel guilty I'm not helping with the cleaning.'

'Don't be. You're at work caring for patients. That's an important job,' Hettie reminded her. 'And I don't think Matron Reed would approve of you coming in here and getting filthy scrubbing floors and walls on your break.'

'Thank you both for giving up your Sunday afternoon to help us. Ned and I appreciate it.'

'We know and we're all glad to help you,' Thea said.

'Ada told us you're meeting her this afternoon.' Hettie dunked her cloth in a bucket of soapy water, then twisted it expertly to wring out the excess water. 'She popped in earlier to see what we were up to and approved of our work!' Hettie chuckled. 'I think she's looking forward to helping you find what you need to furnish the place. There must be loads of things up in the attics going back years and years.'

'We're lucky her Ladyship offered – otherwise I don't know where we would have got what we need.' Evie checked her watch again. 'I must go – I don't want to be late for Ada. I'll see you at Rookery House later.'

After calling a quick goodbye to Ned, Flo and the children, Evie left the old grooms' rooms and hurried back to the Hall where she'd arranged to meet Ada in the servants' quarters. From there they'd go up to the third floor where they could access the attics.

∽

After climbing up three flights of servants' stairs, Evie and Ada paused to catch their breaths.

'Whatever you choose for your new home must go down those stairs.' Ada gestured to the stairwell they had just come up, which was narrower than the main staircase in the Hall and turned in dog-leg bends. 'Matron Reed wouldn't be happy having dusty furniture carried out through the middle of her clean hospital, making a mess and disturbing the patients.'

Evie chuckled. 'I can imagine her reaction if we tried! But she'd be quite correct; we shouldn't disrupt the hospital, that wouldn't do at all. I will just take care to choose things in the attic that we can get down the servants' stairs.'

'This way then.' Ada led her along the corridor past doors that led into rooms where some nurses and other staff slept, and where Evie had stayed occasionally when heavy snow had made getting to and from Rookery House difficult. At the end of the corridor, Ada took a key out of her apron pocket and used it to open a door Evie had barely noticed before, which opened to reveal another, narrower flight of stairs.

'It's all up here,' Ada said, going ahead of Evie.

The sight that met Evie as she reached the top of the narrow stairs made her gasp. The large attic spread out before them, April light shining in from windows on either side of the sloping roof, illuminating dust motes dancing in the air. The attic appeared to stretch the entire length of this central part of the Hall and was packed with an Aladdin's Cave of curious things.

'There's a lot up here.' Ada took a piece of paper from her apron pocket and unfolded it. 'I wrote a list of items I thought you might want for setting up your first home. Best to focus on them. Otherwise you can spend hours up here and get quite distracted. So, I thought, for your kitchen, you need a table, chairs, a cupboard, shelves, crockery, cutlery and cooking utensils.'

Evie listened as Ada reeled off things she'd already thought of herself, but it was good to hear someone else's ideas as well.

'We'd like a bookcase too, if there are any. Ned and I both have a lot of books. Are all of those things on your list stored here?'

'Yes, if you know where to find them,' Ada said. 'I've been up and had a scout around and found some things that you might like. My first time up here was searching out fabric for Marianne to make clothes for her Ladyship and to donate to the clothing depot. That helped me get to know what's where. It is a treasure trove of a place and will help set you up nicely. I remember what it's like moving into your married home for the first time,' Ada said wistfully.

'Was that the cottage you lived in before you came to Rookery House for a while?' Evie asked, recalling when Ada had shared a room with Hettie because her home had been requisitioned as it stood on land that was to be turned into RAF Great Plumstead.

'Yes, Walter and I lived there all our married life. I was there for forty-six years. I still miss it.' A film of tears shone in Ada's eyes before she blinked them away.

Evie reached out and touched the older woman's arm. 'It's been hard for you.'

Ada took out a handkerchief, unfolded it and blew her nose. 'But life goes on. I had to pick up the pieces and start again.' She managed a smile. 'I'm happy here with my job and living at the Hall. It's given me a new purpose. Now, we've got work to do. I don't want Matron after me for keeping you too long on your break. How much time have you got?'

Evie checked her watch. 'I'm due back on duty in three quarters of an hour.'

'Then let's get to work.'

With Ada's knowledge of what was where, they found all they needed, ticking items off on the list as they moved them to a space near the door where they would stay until Evie's day off next Thursday.

'Two single beds aren't ideal, but they will suffice,' Ada said as they carried a second dusty metal bedframe and stacked it on top of the first one.

'They'll be fine. We can tie them together and once there's a double sheet over the two mattresses, you won't be able to tell the difference,' Evie said. She was glad they'd found two single mattresses in decent condition, which had been stored under dustsheets to protect them. Once they were downstairs and outside, she would give them a good beating and sponge down to clear any dirt.

'Reuben's offered to help Ned carry the furniture and things downstairs next Thursday and I'll give it all a thorough clean before we move it into the grooms' rooms. I'm delighted we've found it all.'

Evie surveyed what they'd got. It was everything they needed to set up home, from rugs for the floors to saucepans and bed linen. 'Thank you so much for your help, Ada. I couldn't have done this without you. I'd have got lost up here!'

Ada's cheeks grew pink. 'You're welcome. If you find there's anything else you need once you've settled in, then let me know.'

'Thank you. I'm going to take this lot back home with me,' Evie said, picking up a pile of bedding – sheets, pillowcases and blankets. 'They'll need washing.'

'I'll bring these curtains down for you.' Ada picked up the pairs of curtains that they'd found neatly packed in a trunk. 'These will look lovely once they've been shortened to fit the windows. I doubt very much that the grooms' rooms will ever have looked as nice before.'

'I hope you'll come and have tea with me once we've moved in and then you can see how everything goes together,' Evie offered.

'I'd like that very much,' Ada said. 'Thank you.'

CHAPTER 14

'Next week! That's absolutely wonderful!' Alice exclaimed enthusiastically, her voice carrying along the telephone wires all the way from Yorkshire after Prue told her about her planned visit during their regular Sunday afternoon call.

Prue smiled at her daughter's delighted reaction. 'Will you be able to have some time off? I'm hoping we can do something together?'

'I'll have a word with the Sergeant but I'm hopeful she'll give me a pass. Have you booked a hotel?'

'There's no need, I'm going to be staying with Caroline, a friend of Lady Campbell-Gryce. She lives not far from York Minster. Lady Campbell-Gryce kindly offered for me to accompany her and use the trip as a chance to see you,' Prue said, telling her daughter the parts of the plan that she could, while leaving out the other reason for the journey north.

'It's bound to be a nice house if she's a friend of Lady Campbell-Gryce,' Alice said, sounding impressed. 'It will be lovely for you to stay somewhere like that, Ma. You work so hard and deserve a holiday. I'm looking forward to showing you around York – it's such a lovely place, even though it was hit by a Baedeker raid like Norwich was.'

They talked for a few more minutes before Alice's money ran out and they said a swift goodbye. Prue would telephone Alice at the aerodrome when she arrived in York so she could give her daughter a contact telephone number for where she was staying.

Replacing the receiver on its cradle, Prue was excited at the thought of seeing her daughter soon. She still missed her despite it being more than a year since Alice had left to join the WAAF. It was impossible for Prue to see either of her sons, with Edwin somewhere in North Africa and Jack in the north of England so the prospect of spending time with at least one of her children filled Prue with joy. But that wasn't until next week and, in the meantime, there was plenty of work to be done.

~

'Afternoon missus!' Percy Blake called out, pausing in his digging as Prue walked past the end of his allotment. 'Lovely day for getting on with some growing.'

'Good afternoon, Percy. It is indeed.' She threw him a smile, thinking how different his behaviour towards her and the other women who worked on the village's Women's Institute allotment was now, compared with when they'd first taken over their plot. Back then, Percy and some of his fellow allotment holder friends, all of them men, had been scathing and doubted the women's ability to grow anything at all. Prue recalled how when Percy had commented that the women were like old hens scratching about in the earth, he'd quickly received short shrift from Gloria. Since then, the women had more than proven themselves with their commitment, hard work and ability, turning the former bramble, dock and nettle-filled patch of land into a very successful allotment.

Continuing towards the WI plot, Prue spotted the familiar figure of Gloria already at work, wearing the pair of colourful, flower-patterned dungarees that she'd made to wear while she worked there. Not for the first time, Prue thought how refreshing and delightful it was to have someone like Gloria in the village. With her bottle-blonde pompadour hairstyle, which this afternoon was wrapped in a fuchsia pink scarf, and her colourful style of dressing, she'd stood out like a bright bird of paradise when she'd arrived in the autumn of 1939 with a trainload of other expectant evacuee mothers. Her bright, individual style had been a sharp contrast to the more conservative muted colours worn by the village women – and Prue loved it.

'You're hard at work already,' Prue said as she reached Gloria, who was crouched down planting some of the seed potatoes which had sprouted green shoots.

Gloria stood up and rubbed the small of her back. 'Dora went down for 'er nap early so I thought I'd best get on while I could. Trying to do this with a three-year-old ain't so easy as doing it on me own! Sylvia's keeping an eye on Dora and will bring 'er along 'ere when she wakes up,' Gloria explained, referring to the landlady she was billeted with who had, after some initial troubles, become one of Gloria's firmest friends.

'Then I'd best join you so we can get the potatoes in quick.'

'There's still plenty left to plant.' Gloria pointed at the three full wooden boxes she'd left at one end of the area they'd assigned for growing potatoes this year. 'Should be another good crop.'

'Let's hope so. I'll grab a trowel from the shed and get started,' Prue said.

Working alongside Gloria, Prue found the task of planting

the potatoes a soothing one. First, she dug a hole in the rich brown soil, which they'd prepared well over the past few weeks, digging in well-rotted manure to help give a good yield, then gently placed a potato in, green sprouts pointing upwards, before she covered it over then moved on and repeated the process.

'I'm going on a trip next week,' Prue said.

'Where to? Anywhere nice?' Gloria asked, glancing up from her planting.

'To York. I'm going to see Alice.'

'That'll be lovely for you both. I know 'ow much you miss 'er, don't yer?'

Prue nodded. 'I do. I'm going on Wednesday and back on Monday. Would you be able to cover my shift at The Mother's Day Club on Friday, please?'

'Of course, and what about your route for the Pie Scheme on Monday?' Gloria asked. 'I could do that for you as well. Dora would love going out to deliver the pies instead of us staying in the village and manning the pie stall. It would make a lovely change.'

'Would you? That's really kind of you, Gloria, thank you.'

Gloria reached out a soil-dusted hand and touched Prue's arm. 'If there's anyone in this village who deserves some time off it's you, Prue. You're always on the go doing things for other people, so 'onestly, I'm glad to be able to 'elp you.'

'I appreciate it. It's almost a year since Victor died and I think it will be good for Alice and me to spend some time in each other's company. She took his death hard. She knew what he was like but still...' Prue lifted a shoulder.

'He was 'er father and she's a kind-'earted girl,' Gloria said sympathetically. 'She loved 'im. Seeing you will 'elp take the sting out of it a bit.'

'I hope so. I know it will do *me* good to see her.' Prue

paused for a moment. 'It doesn't seem long since she was the same age as your Dora… they grow up so fast.'

'You 'ave to make the most of it when they're small,' Gloria said, placing a potato in the hole she'd just dug. 'Even though your Alice is all grown up she's still your daughter, but in a different way. She still needs you.'

'I'm very proud of what she's done, leaving home and joining the WAAF. Spreading her wings and going to different places, meeting new people and learning important skills for her job. I'm not sure I would have been brave enough to do that,' Prue admitted.

Gloria stared at Prue for a moment before letting out a throaty chuckle. 'Not brave enough?! You are one of the bravest women I know, Prue. Look at all you do around this village, the people you sort out and stand up to. This place and plenty of people in it would be a lot worse off without your spirit, determination and bravery.'

'I don't…' Prue began.

'Well, I *do* know,' Gloria said determinedly. 'So don't put yourself down. Now, brave you may be – but you still need to get those potatoes planted.' She wriggled her finely-shaped eyebrows at Prue and pointed her trowel at the sprouted potatoes still nestling in the box beside them. 'Come on, let's get on with it before a certain three-year-old arrives and wants to join in!'

Prue let out a hearty laugh and got back to work.

CHAPTER 15

Marianne pushed the pram, in which Bea lay sleeping, in through the gate of Rookery House, while the older children charged off around the side of the house heading for the back door. She'd spent the afternoon at a session of The Mother's Day Club with her daughters and, afterwards, they'd met George and Betty from school and all walked home together. Emily had been delighted, walking all the way back to Rookery House hand in hand with her two friends, whom she missed when they were at school. No doubt the three of them were hungry and hoping Hettie would have something waiting for them to eat, Marianne thought following them around to the rear of the house.

After parking the pram in the scullery, Marianne left Bea to sleep for a little longer and went into the kitchen where the children were now seated at the table. Each of them was tucking into a slice of Hettie's freshly made bread spread generously with creamy butter.

'I washed my hands, Mummy.' Emily held up her free hand,

turning it around to show both the palm and back before taking another bite of her bread and butter.

'So did we.' Betty held up one of her hands and nudged her brother, who sat beside her, to do the same.

'I'm glad to hear it. They all look lovely and clean.' Marianne met Hettie's gaze and the older woman winked, a look of amusement on her face.

'Did you have a good afternoon at The Mother's Day Club?' Hettie asked Marianne.

'Yes, we did. We managed to get a lot more work done for the clothing depot.' Marianne took off her coat and hung it on one of the pegs near the door. 'Are Thea and Flo about?'

'I'll be making them some tea shortly. Flo's in the greenhouse and Thea's tending her chicks – she does take such special care of them.'

'We help as well,' said Betty and George nodded with his mouth full.

'There's a letter come for you in the afternoon post,' Hettie told Marianne. 'I've left it there for you.' She gestured towards the large brown envelope lying on the dresser.

Marianne's heart lifted. 'Oh good, it must be this month's edition of *The Prisoner of War*.' She hurried across and opened the envelope, pulling out the journal that was sent to each POW's next of kin with information, reports about camps and even photographs of prisoners in it. It was a precious way of discovering what life might be like for Alex. He was limited in what he could say in his letters, although she suspected that, even if he could say more, he would spare her any details that would make her worry further about him.

'Come on you three, why don't we go out and have a look at Auntie Thea's new chicks, see how they're doing?' Hettie suggested. 'You can bring your bread and butter with you, eat it as we go along.'

Without needing to be asked twice, the three children left their seats at the table, taking what was left of their snack with them. 'Wait for me by the door,' Hettie instructed them before lowering her voice and turning to Marianne. 'I'll keep them outside for a bit, give you a chance to have a look through the journal, just in case… you know.'

'Thanks, Hettie.' Marianne gave her friend a grateful smile, knowing that the older woman understood how much she valued the journal and that each time a new one arrived it brought her hope that Alex might be in one of the photos of the men taken in the camps. When each issue came Marianne scanned the pages first, hoping for a glimpse of her husband, no matter how small or how grainy the black and white image might be. Anything that would help to fill the gap of not seeing him. It had been almost eighteen months since he'd last been on leave, right before he was shot down over enemy territory.

Once she was alone, Marianne sat down at the table and began to look through the journal. As usual the first page started with 'The Editor Writes' and Marianne's eyes skimmed briefly over the words, knowing that she would come back and read them properly later. As much as she wanted to rush through the pages searching for Alex's face among the photos, Marianne forced herself to slow down. The anticipation was bittersweet. So far, Alex hadn't been in the journal – not even his camp had featured – but there was always the possibility, and that hope, that maybe, made her heartbeat quicken.

She slowly turned the next page and saw an article about the different jobs that POWs did while out on working parties. She didn't read it, just studied the photos but didn't recognise any of the men. The next page raised her hopes, with a collection of photos of men at different camps, posing in groups of up to thirty or forty, each image labelled as 'Stalag' for German camps or 'Campo' for Italian ones. But none of them were Alex's camp. Perhaps on another page, Marianne thought, keeping her hopes up. As she worked her way through the pages there were more images of POWs but none of them was her husband.

Reaching the final page, Marianne tried not to let her disappointment overwhelm her. She firmly reminded herself that there were thousands of POWs so the chance of Alex being in a photo was small. Some families, who like her had received their copy of the journal today, would be thrilled to see their son, husband or father's picture in this issue and Marianne was pleased for them. Unfortunately, today wasn't that day for her. Perhaps next month.

Rather than sit and dwell and wish for something she couldn't change, or had no control over, Marianne got up from the table and put the journal safely on the dresser to read through later after her girls had gone to bed. In the meantime, she needed to wake Bea up or she wouldn't go to sleep properly later. She'd take her outside and go and join the others.

With a still sleepy and slightly grumpy Bea in her arms, Marianne made her way to where Hettie, Thea and the three children were gathered around the moveable chicken run watching the nine gorgeous little chicks with their soft, pale brown downy feathers. The chicks were darting around investigating the grass and picking at things, watched over by their clucking, ever attentive mother.

'Come and see, Mummy and Bea,' Emily beckoned to them as they drew near. 'Look at the baby chicks.'

Bea wriggled in Marianne's arms to be put down and she

joined the other children crouched by the run. 'You must be quiet,' Emily warned her sister in a loud whisper. 'We mustn't upset the mother hen or her babies.'

A loud *tuk-tuk* noise came from the hen as she found a morsel for them to eat in the grass, her call bringing some of the chicks rushing to her side, making the children laugh.

Hettie caught Marianne's eye and raised her eyebrows questioningly.

Marianne shook her head.

'Maybe next month, eh?' Hettie said.

Thea touched Marianne's arm and gave her a sympathetic smile.

'Maybe. Or the month after; sometime, I hope. In the meantime, we need to keep carrying on, don't we?'

'We do, and making the most of each day and the good things in it helps. Things like these lovely chicks,' Hettie said. 'They're one of the joys of springtime, of new life and hope.'

Marianne smiled at her friends, then crouched down next to her daughters, delighted by the joy on their faces as they watched the chicks. She would write about this to Alex tonight, help keep him part of his daughters' lives. Despite Alex being far away, they were still a family and would be reunited some day. Until then, she would make the best of things.

CHAPTER 16

As the train puffed its way through the rainy Norfolk countryside, leaving Great Plumstead far behind, Prue decided she'd waited long enough – it was time to head to the first class carriage. She took her suitcase down from the overhead rack and made her way from the compartment, which apart from her was unoccupied, and then along the corridor towards the front of the train.

Prue had seen Lady Campbell-Gryce get into the first class carriage back at Great Plumstead station. As planned, they hadn't spoken or even looked at each other before boarding. Whilst Prue had waited at the far end of the platform, her Ladyship had stayed in the waiting room until the train arrived, when the porter had carried her suitcase to the train for her.

They'd given no indication that they were heading off on a mission together. There was nothing for any of the village gossips to chew over, to wonder and imagine what Lady Campbell-Gryce and Prue Wilson might be up to. Prue smiled at the thought. If only they knew!

Arriving in the first class carriage, Prue glanced into the compartments searching for her Ladyship and was struck by the differences to the second class one in which she usually travelled. The seats were wider, more comfortable and covered with plusher fabric. Reaching the end compartment she found Lady Campbell-Gryce sitting on her own. She gave a small knock, then slid open the door and went in.

Her Ladyship looked up and gave Prue a welcoming smile. 'Prue, come in!' She gestured for her to take the seat opposite her next to the window.

Prue stowed her suitcase in the overhead rack, then sat down facing Lady Campbell-Gryce. 'We're on our way. Is everything still as you planned?'

'It is. Anthony is due in York tomorrow evening and will be staying at the Royal Station Hotel, so Caroline has informed me. He's meeting *his mistress* there at seven o'clock – and we'll be there too, ready and waiting.'

'Lady Campbell-Gryce…' Prue began but halted as the other woman reached forward and patted Prue's arm.

'Please call me Clemmie, the same as my other friends do.' She leaned back against her seat, regarding Prue. 'You and I have shared significant confidences, things that I haven't even spoken about to most of my oldest friends. You are one of the few people I could ask to help me with this task of mine. I trust you, Prue, and know that you understand. So please, no more Lady Campbell-Gryce or your Ladyship. Just call me Clemmie from now on.'

Prue nodded, smiling. 'Very well then, Clemmie it is. What I was going to say was, are you still sure you want to go through with confronting your husband? It's not that I don't think it's a good idea, but I'm worried in case it goes wrong, and you don't get the outcome you want.'

'I appreciate you challenging me on that. And believe you

me, it's certainly something I've thought about a great deal in the dark hours of the night when I can't sleep.' Clemmie glanced out of the window at the passing countryside for a moment before returning her attention to Prue. 'The truth is *I don't know* if it will work, but if I don't try then I know I'll regret it. If I do nothing, then he may be persuaded to end our marriage and destroy our family to be with her. If I confront him, then he may still do that, but I think there is a chance it will bring him to his senses. I want to make him realise what he has to lose and question if his mistress is really worth it.' She let out a soft sigh. 'So yes, I'm very much intending to go ahead with my mission – and I'm aiming for the best outcome.'

'I hope it works out well for you, I really do,' Prue said.

She felt for Clemmie and the way her future hung in the balance. At least with Victor gone Prue no longer had the worry about where his relationship with his mistress might lead. Had he not been killed in the Norwich Blitz, but survived and gone on to end their marriage, then Prue would have had a lot less to lose than Clemmie did. In fact, Prue would have been relieved to be free of Victor. Clemmie's situation was far more serious and Prue was sure she was doing the right thing to embark on this attempt, risky as it was, to hold her marriage together.

'Now, are you hungry?' Clemmie asked. 'By the weight of it, Mrs Shepherd, our cook, has provided me with a picnic with very generous portions, enough to last me all the way to York – and back again!' She turned to the basket that sat on the seat beside her and folded back the gingham cloth that had been neatly covering it. 'There are sandwiches, some of her delicious cheese scones… we have a bottle of cordial and a flask of tea. And if I am not mistaken…' She removed a waxed paper packet and undid one end. 'Aha, yes. Two slices of her exceptional apple cake. Where shall we begin? On school jollies, I always started with cake.' She met Prue's eyes, a sweetly nostalgic expression on her face. 'But I suppose we must keep up standards. How about a sandwich first, cake after?'

'Sounds delicious, thank you.'

'Super.' Clemmie pulled out two waxed paper packets which had been labelled in pencil. 'Beetroot and cheese or potted meat? I know, let's both have half of each. It will be rather like a midnight feast at boarding school,' she added as she unwrapped the sandwiches.

'I've never been to a midnight feast,' Prue said, regretfully. 'I only went to the village school and was at home with my parents otherwise. Though there was mischief to be had, what with Thea, Reuben and especially our little sister Lizzie leading us astray!'

Clemmie regarded Prue with the raise of an eyebrow as she handed her half of the sandwiches in waxed paper. 'Then I suspect you were a great deal happier than I was, because the *only* good things about my boarding school, apart from friends like Caroline, were days out by train to the theatre and midnight feasts.' She gave Prue a wry smile. 'Luckily, we now have no risk at all of being caught sharing our food by a house matron, or any teachers, bursting rudely in and stopping the fun. So let's tuck in!'

Arriving at York station several hours later, Prue let out a gasp as she stepped down from the carriage. The bright light streaming on to the platform from above had made her look up and what she saw there brought crashing home yet another of the destructive horrors of wartime. Much of the station's roof was simply gone, leaving just the arched steel girders like bare rib bones silhouetted against the sky. She knew this was the work of another Baedeker raid last spring, the day after the first one had hit Norwich.

'Gosh!' Clemmie exclaimed, staring up at the destruction. 'Caroline told me in a letter about what happened here but seeing it for oneself is shocking.'

'It is a shock,' agreed Prue. 'City Station in Norwich was badly damaged, but that isn't anywhere near as big as this place.' She cast her gaze around the large station. Only some buildings remained standing and functional but the platforms were busy with trains and passengers.

'Thankfully the trains can still run here,' Clemmie said. 'Let's find a taxi to take us to Caroline's.'

Outside the entrance to the station, Clemmie flagged down a taxi and they climbed in with their luggage.

'Where to?' the driver asked, turning his head slightly towards them.

'Bootham Terrace please,' Clemmie said as she settled back in the seat.

'Right you are,' the driver acknowledged and started the engine.

As they pulled out of the station forecourt and onto the road, Prue noticed the city wall, built of grey stone on top of a high grassy bank, running off in two directions. The ancient wall was medieval, Alice had told her, and it was still in good condition and circled the city. Prue was looking forward to investigating it some more with her daughter.

'There's the Royal Station Hotel.' Clemmie pointed to a large building to their left, not far from the station, as they drove past.

Prue craned her neck around to look out the back window of the taxi. The hotel looked impressive – exactly the sort of place Lord Campbell-Gryce would stay.

As if picking up on Prue's thoughts, Clemmie said in a low voice, 'It's near the station so convenient for him on his travels for the War Office, as well as being suitably discreet for his other needs...'

The rest of the journey passed quickly with Prue looking out of the window and Clemmie pointing out landmarks to her such as the River Ouse, as they crossed over it on one of the many bridges, and the towering York Minster, the city's cathedral.

'Whereabouts?' the taxi driver asked as he slowed and turned into Bootham Terrace.

'Halfway down,' Clemmie instructed. 'Number fourteen.'

After the taxi driver had dropped them off, Prue stood on the pavement staring up at the grand house before her. It was five storeys high, had large bay windows facing out onto the street and a small front garden surrounded by a low wall and iron railing fence. Prue could feel a flutter of nerves. She was not used to meeting people from Clemmie's class – let alone staying in their house. Would she get along with Caroline as easily as she was finding it with Clemmie?

'Here we are then.' Clemmie picked up her suitcase and the basket with the remains of their picnic. 'Our home for the next few days. Come and meet Caroline.'

Prue followed Clemmie in through the iron gate and up the flight of five stone steps leading to the black front door, which flew open before they could knock.

'Clemmie!' A tall, slim woman in a green dress and with wavy auburn hair cut into a jaw-length bob threw her arms around Clemmie, hugging her tightly. 'I'm so glad to see you here.' Then quickly releasing her, she turned her attention to Prue, holding out her hand. 'Welcome, Prue. I understand you are a fellow member of the WVS.' She indicated her own green uniform dress.

'Hello, yes I am,' Prue said politely, shaking Caroline's hand rather formally.

Caroline used her free hand to give Prue's arm a friendly squeeze. 'Then we must compare notes while you're here, swap ideas,' she said enthusiastically. 'Come inside, we'll get you settled in – it's my pleasure to have you both here!'

'Isn't she a wonderful, warm person?' Clemmie confided to Prue as Caroline led them into the long, bright hallway.

'Yes, she is,' replied Prue, feeling a wave of calm and relief. She'd liked Caroline instantly!

CHAPTER 17

Usually on her day off, Evie would sleep later, have a leisurely breakfast and then slowly catch up with all the things she didn't have time to do on the days when she was working long shifts at the hospital. Things like her washing, writing to her mother and cleaning and tidying the room she shared with Flo. But not today.

She'd been awake with the sun, come downstairs, lit the fire under the copper to heat water and made other preparations for washing the bed linen that she'd brought back from the attics of Great Plumstead Hall on Sunday.

Hettie, who'd come down soon after Evie to start preparing breakfast for everyone, had kindly offered to wash them for her, but Evie had politely turned her down. So far her long shifts at the hospital hadn't allowed Evie to do much work at all preparing her and Ned's new home, but now she had a chance to get cracking – starting with washing the bed linen as soon as breakfast was over.

With everyone else now up and seated at the table eating their breakfast, Evie scooped up the last spoonful of her porridge and glanced out of the window, relieved that yesterday's rain had blown over to give a day of spring sunshine with a breeze. It was perfect for drying washing.

'You all set and ready to do your laundry?' Hettie asked from her seat at the end of the table, as Evie got up and placed her empty bowl at the sink.

'I think so. I should be able to get it all finished and on the line by late morning and then I'll head up to the Hall to clean the furniture. Mr White has given Ned an hour off to carry it down from the attic and Reuben's said he'll give him a hand,' Evie said.

'Do you want me to come and help too?' Thea offered.

'Thank you, but I'll be fine, and you have plenty to do here.'

'*We* could have a day off,' Betty piped up. 'We can scrub floors again, can't we George? We like it.'

George looked up at Thea with a hopeful expression.

'I think Miss Carter might have something to say about you missing her lovely lessons,' Thea said. 'And isn't your class getting ready for maypole dancing? You'll not want to miss that.'

'No, we won't!' said George.

'But we *are* good at scrubbing,' Betty insisted.

'You both did an excellent job,' Evie assured them. 'The kitchen floor is spick and span! But school is too important – and fun – so I can't possibly let you miss it. Thank you for the kind offer, though. How about the next time we're scrubbing floors, I come and get you? Just not on school days.'

Betty and George both seemed satisfied, and Evie gave them a smile before heading off to the scullery to begin her work.

Evie was glad she'd pinned up her auburn hair and wrapped a scarf around her head, turban style with the knot at the front, as it was hot, heavy work washing the bed linen.

First, she'd washed the sheets in hot soapy water, using the wooden dolly to move them around in the big metal tub, then she'd transferred them to the copper to boil wash. After that she'd rinsed them in clean water, followed by another rinse with a blue bag in the water to bring them up even whiter. Now she was on the last stage, feeding the folded clean white sheets through the mangle to squeeze out water before she hung them on the line outside to dry.

Turning the handle of the mangle's wheel, Evie thought about how different her life was now from the one she used to have. Then, all her washing was done by someone else – she never scrubbed a floor or had to clean or tidy her home. It had been like that all her life, from the moment she was born until she'd finally upped and left Douglas. She'd grown up in a well-off home, had a privileged schooling and married into a very wealthy family.

These days Evie was no stranger to hard physical work. Many of the tasks she did regularly at the hospital had her using her muscles to scrub and clean and move patients or furniture around. And now, as she washed the bed linen ready for her new home, she was quite content and wouldn't change a thing, because her life was, at last, a happy one.

Once all the cleaned bedding had been through the mangle, Evie carried it outside in the large wicker washing basket, remembering to grab the peg bag from its hook just inside the scullery door.

The Rookery House washing lines were strung up between sturdy posts and criss-crossed an area of lawn to the south-facing side of the house, where the sun would shine directly on them for most of the day.

One by one Evie hung each item, pegging it securely in place. Once she'd finished, she stepped back and felt a swell of satisfaction as the sheets, pillowcases and blankets caught in a sudden breeze, billowing and snapping as the fabric danced on the lines.

'They should dry well today.' Evie turned around to see Hettie coming from the direction of the orchard with a basket full of brown speckled eggs. 'I'll get it in for you later,' she added.

Evie opened her mouth to protest but before she could, Hettie reminded her, 'You'll be up at the Hall sorting out there. It won't take me five minutes to get this lot in once it's dry.'

'Thanks, Hettie. I was concerned that it might come on to rain by the time I got back. I won't have to worry now I know you're keeping an eye on things.'

'At the first sniff of rain,' Hettie agreed, 'I'll have them in.'

∼

Pedalling up the long drive to Great Plumstead Hall, heading into the strengthening wind, Evie was glad she was wearing the pair of dungarees Flo had loaned her. They had no skirt to blow around like her nurse's uniform did and so were warmer, as well as being far more practical for the work she had to do today. In fact, they would be ideal for her nursing work too, although she doubted Matron Reed would ever think so.

Bicycling across the wide sweep of gravel in front of the Hall, Evie steered around the back to the courtyard as she always did when arriving for work. She braked, came to a halt and dismounted and it suddenly dawned on her that soon this wouldn't just be her place of work but where she lived too. It was going to be her and Ned's home. A tingle of excitement fizzed through her. Each thing Ned, their friends or she did in preparation was a step closer. Washing the bed linen from the attics was a step. And now Evie was about to do another. Step by step they were getting there.

As arranged, Ned and Reuben, who was Thea's brother, along with another young lad who worked at Home Farm, arrived at midday to carry down the things they needed from Great Plumstead Hall's attic.

'It's three flights up and then another shorter one,' Evie warned them as they began to climb the first flight of servants' stairs.

'Just as well we're carrying things down rather than up,' Reuben observed wryly.

'Cook has offered to give you all a meal afterwards if you'd like one,' Evie said. 'Restore your energy levels before you go back to work.'

'That sounds good.' Ned winked at her as he climbed the stairs beside her. 'Better than sandwiches. You both up for that too?' He directed this question to Reuben and the young lad.

'Definitely,' Reuben said.

'Yes, please,' the lad said, shyly.

'Then I'll let her know after I go down with my first load,' Evie said.

Finally reaching the attic, the men surveyed the furniture and other items that Evie and Ada had selected and left in the space near the doorway.

'Shall we start by taking a bed frame down between us?' Ned gestured to Reuben. 'And if you can take one of the mattresses?' he asked the lad.

Evie looked around and spotted some rugs rolled up which she could manage. 'I'll take those and on my way back up I'll bring some baskets to carry the kitchen things.'

'Mind how you go on the stairs everyone,' Reuben said,

picking up one end of the metal bed frame while Ned took the other. Then they manoeuvred it slowly and carefully out through the doorway and down the narrow stairs to the next floor.

The lad heaved a mattress up and over his shoulders and, with his head bent under it, followed them.

Left on her own, Evie gathered up four rolled-up rugs in her arms and began her own descent. She could hear Reuben and Ned below her, calling out instructions to one another as they negotiated the bed frame around the dog-leg turns in the stairs. By the time she was down, Ned, Reuben and the lad were ready to head back up.

'We've left the frame and mattress in the courtyard to clean,' Ned told her.

'Thank you. I'll be back up in minute or two.'

Evie left the rugs leaning against the wall just inside the back door and popped into the kitchen to tell Cook the men would like some food afterwards. Cook lent her two wicker baskets and, with these in hand, she began the climb up to the attic once more.

One step at a time, she told herself. And realising the irony of her words, she laughed.

'You all right, Evie?' Ned called down.

'Never better!' she replied, grinning from ear to ear.

∽

It was almost one o'clock by the time everything had been brought down from the attic. Most of it was in the courtyard ready for Evie's attention, apart from a few things like the cooking utensils and crockery which had been left in the corridor near the Hall's kitchen.

'Time for some food,' Evie said, ushering Ned, Reuben and

the lad into the servants' hall. With its long table and benches, it was now used as a dining room for the mobile patients, but they'd already eaten their midday meal and returned to the main part of the hospital. One of the kitchen assistants was clearing away their used plates and cutlery. She looked up as they came in. 'Are you ready for your meal?'

'Yes, please,' Ned said as they sat down at the table. 'We've quite an appetite after going up and down those stairs.'

'I'll be right back with your food,' the kitchen assistant said, carrying a loaded tray of used crockery out of the room.

'What's your next job?' Reuben said.

'Cleaning everything,' Evie said. 'I'm glad it's still good weather – I can wash and beat and dust it all outside in the courtyard and things will dry. It's a suntrap out there and warms up nicely. Cook's said I can use the scullery to wash all the kitchen things.'

'I'm still painting the rooms,' Ned told Reuben. 'Doing a bit each night.'

'We're hoping to be able to move in on my day off next week,' Evie said. 'Fingers crossed.'

'Here we are.' The kitchen assistant returned with four plates of shepherd's pie and cabbage, and then fetched a tray with cutlery and tumblers of elderflower cordial.

'Thank you,' everyone said.

'This looks good,' Reuben said, picking up his knife and fork ready to eat. 'I'm happy to come along and shift furniture for you again if I'm going to be rewarded with a good meal like this!'

Evie laughed. 'I'll remember that if we need more things brought down from the attic.'

∽

After Ned, Reuben and the lad had returned to their workplaces, Evie began her task of cleaning the furniture in the courtyard. She moved the mattresses against a wall and gave them a good beating with a carpet beater to remove dust, and then sponged them down and left them in the sunshine to dry.

Next, she turned her attention to the bed frames and scrubbed them with hot soapy water, just as she'd done in the hospital so many times before. Then she moved on to removing the drawers from the chest of drawers and wiping them out with a wet soapy cloth before propping them up against a wall in the sun. After that she washed down the outer parts of the chest of drawers. All the while she hummed as she worked, happy to be doing this towards her new home.

By the end of the afternoon, Evie was tired but delighted to have rugs with the dust beaten out of them hanging on the washing line strung across the courtyard to air, and squeaky-clean crockery, cutlery, kitchen utensils and pots and pans, that she'd washed in the Hall's large scullery sink, drying on the drainer.

'It looks so much better!' Ned said, surveying the fruits of her labour when he came to see her after he'd finished work at five. 'You've worked miracles, Evie!'

'I'll bring some of Hettie's beeswax and lavender polish and give all the wooden furniture a polishing next week, after we've moved in,' Evie said.

Ned put his arms around her and pulled her to him. 'I'm counting the days till then. It's going to be wonderful having our own home together.'

Evie met his loving gaze. 'Seven days to go and counting! Right, let's get this lot moved into the grooms' rooms – it can't stay out here. We'll put most of it in the kitchen for now, since you've finished painting in there, and then we can sort everything out properly and decide what goes where, next Thursday.'

They began to move the now clean furniture, rugs and kitchen things into what was to be their new home. This was yet another step closer to her and Ned being able to move in, Evie thought. It had been a long and hard day's work – but she'd loved every minute of it.

CHAPTER 18

Hettie stretched the dough, folding it over and repeating the process, working in the steady kneading rhythm she loved. It gave her time to think and ponder, or just be, enjoying the quiet calm of bread making. It was a job she always enjoyed. She was alone in the house this morning, with Marianne and the girls at The Mother's Day Club in the village, George and Betty at school, Thea out with the WVS canteen and Flo and Nancy outside working in the garden.

After giving the dough a final knead she placed it in the large ceramic bowl, covered it with a clean cloth and placed it by the stove to rise in the warmth. Hettie was washing her hands at the sink when a familiar figure passed by the kitchen window and moments later opened the back door and stepped inside.

'Morning, Ada.' Hettie greeted her older sister. 'You've timed that well. I was just about to stop for a cuppa while the dough rises. Do you have time for one?'

'Morning.' Ada gave a nod of her head. 'I do, thank you.' She took off her coat and laid it tidily over the back of one of the chairs around the large table standing in the middle of the kitchen. 'I've been into the village and thought I'd call and see how you are.'

'I'm fine. Busy as usual but that's the way I like it.' Hettie went over to the stove and pushed the kettle onto the hotplate to come up to the boil, then started to prepare the cups and teapot, spooning in fresh tea leaves. 'How about yourself?'

'I'm well, thank you. Her Ladyship's gone away for a few days, same as his Lordship, so there's no one to look after at the Hall. Not that I shall be doing nothing you understand. There are always things to be done.' Ada pulled out a chair and sat down.

'Even so, you should enjoy these few days of quiet,' Hettie said, taking the kettle off the hotplate after it had quickly come to the boil and pouring hot water into the teapot. 'You could treat yourself to a trip to the pictures in Wykeham. Let it transport you to another place for a while. I'd forgotten how it feels to escape like that.'

'You say that as if you've just been to the pictures yourself.'

'I have. On Saturday. We went to see *The Mask of Zorro* and I loved it!' Hettie chuckled as she sat down in the chair opposite her sister. 'That picture has finished now but there'll be something new on you could see.'

'Who did you go with? Thea and the children?' Ada asked.

'No, with Ted.' Hettie watched as her sister's eyes widened.

'Ted Ellison?' Ada's voice had an edge to it.

'Yes, that's right. He enjoyed it too so we're planning on going again sometime.'

Ada sat quietly for a moment before leaning forward in her chair, her shrewd brown eyes looking into Hettie's. 'What's going on with Ted? Are you two courting?'

Hettie bit her bottom lip to stem the guffaw that threatened to spill out, sensing that now would not be a good time. She knew from experience that her older sister lacked a sense of fun; it was best to always play it straight with her.

'No.' Hettie reached for the teapot and poured them each a cup of tea. 'We're just friends, that's all.'

'Is that what *he* thinks?' Ada probed. 'Or has he got his eye on you to become his next wife?'

Hettie put the teapot down and pulled a knitted tea cosy over it, giving herself a moment rather than coming out with some retort which would end up starting an argument with her sister. 'As far as I'm concerned, Ted is my friend, a good companion of my generation. We enjoy each other's company, that's all.'

Ada pursed her lips. 'But what if he does want to marry you, Hettie? Would you say yes? You ought to be prepared, you know. And not be surprised and whisked away.'

Hettie almost laughed again. What a strange view of things her sister had. And Ada must hardly know her at all. Hettie would not in a million years describe herself as someone who could be whisked away by a man!

She let out a sigh. 'Steady on, Ada. You're putting the cart before the horse. I don't have any plans to marry Ted or anyone else. If he has other ideas then he hasn't said and if he does, then I'll deal with them sensibly, if and when it happens.'

Ada folded her arms across her small birdlike body. 'I'm only looking out for you as your older sister, that's all.'

'I know, but Ted and I are just friends. I don't have any plans for anything more than that.'

'You say that, but other people might get ideas, seeing the pair of you out together,' Ada warned her.

'If they do, then that's their business. I'm not going to let what other people think rule what I do. We've both known Ted for many years and you know as well as I do that he's a good, decent person who is a pleasure to be with.' Hettie stirred some milk into her tea before changing the subject. 'Now, where's Lady Campbell-Gryce gone to? Down to London?'

'I'm not sure – she didn't actually say,' Ada said, frowning. 'It's not like her to not tell me. I suppose she must have forgotten. She hasn't been herself these past couple of weeks. You get to sense these things working for the Campbell-Gryces the way I do.'

Hettie nodded, glad to have her sister on safer ground, happy to talk about her job and employers as if she had worked at the Hall for many years instead of only since the summer of 1941. 'I'm sure her Ladyship can trust you and rely on your discretion,' Hettie said pointedly.

'Of course she can!' Ada snapped. 'I would *never* say a word to anyone else. It's only because you used to work there that I've said anything to you.'

'And it will go no further,' Hettie reassured her sister. 'Perhaps she's worried about her children. With them both in the services it must weigh on her Ladyship's mind, same as any mother who has sons or daughters doing their bit.'

'Something neither of us have the experience of,' Ada said, her tone softening. 'I sometimes wonder what my life would have been like if Walter and I had had children.' She took a sip of her tea. 'But it never happened. Wasn't meant to be I suppose. But then life doesn't always give you what you hope for. I never thought I'd be forced to leave my home to make way for an aerodrome and end up working as housekeeper at the Hall.'

'Life twists and turns in unexpected ways,' Hettie said. 'But you enjoy your job, don't you?'

Ada nodded, her face breaking into a rare smile. 'Yes, I do. It's given me a new role and home at the Hall, just when I needed them. I am more than thankful.'

'I'm glad for you, I really am,' Hettie said. 'It's a change of life that has brought you happiness.'

'None of us knows what's around the corner,' Ada said, still with a smile on her face.

Hettie sighed inwardly. Was she referring again to Hettie's friendship with Ted? She hoped not. There really was nothing more to their relationship than what was plain to see. Though clearly some people were going to imagine there was a lot more to it and draw entirely wrong conclusions. It was something Hettie would have to be ready to endure and put people right about. She only hoped Ted didn't come in for the same comments and questions from the gossips. And if he did, that it wouldn't cause him to put an end to what was becoming a valuable and enjoyable companionship for them both.

CHAPTER 19

Prue's stomach was twisting into knots as she and Clemmie walked in through the front entrance of the Royal Station Hotel a little after half past six. They'd spent the evening after they'd arrived in York, and all the following day, inside Caroline's home in Bootham Terrace, deciding it was best not to venture out in case Clemmie should be spotted by Lord Campbell-Gryce's mistress, who lived in York and who would know Clemmie by sight from the many functions they'd both attended. If Anthony or Lavinia knew Clemmie was in York, they might change or abort their meeting, which would scupper Clemmie's carefully laid plan to confront them together this evening.

'Chin up, old girl,' Clemmie said softly, leaning slightly towards Prue as they headed for the dining room. 'We *can* do this!'

Prue glanced at her friend, who with Caroline's help and some loans from the WVS clothing depot had undergone a transformation and no longer looked like the usual Clemmie. Gone were her beautifully tailored clothes, designed and matched to suit her complexion and hair. Instead, she was wearing a smart but rather dull tweed suit and cream blouse and her hair was fashioned into a chignon. A pair of sensible brown brogues were on her feet and she wore round plain glass spectacles. She had the appearance of the kind of woman a man like Lord Campbell-Gryce wouldn't look twice at, which was exactly what they wanted. Should he glance in their direction, Clemmie needed to blend into the background and remain hidden in full sight while she observed her husband and his mistress.

As for Prue, they'd decided they need not worry about his Lordship recognising her. Although they lived in the same village their paths seldom crossed and she'd never actually spoken to him.

Prue touched Clemmie's elbow. 'Of course we can do this,' she said in an upbeat voice that came out a little more high-pitched than she'd intended. 'We *are* doing it!'

We're both nervous, Prue thought, and rightly so. But we're doing it…

They were seated by the maître-d at a table Caroline had scouted out for them and booked. It was behind a fringe of potted palms and in a spot where they had direct sight of the table where his Lordship always sat by the window. Unlikely to be seen themselves because of the potted palms, it was also positioned in the inner area of the dining room, meaning Anthony – and Lavinia – wouldn't pass by to get to Anthony's table.

As planned, Clemmie sat with her back to the table Anthony and his mistress were due to occupy shortly. Prue was to be her eyes and act as observer. She would tell her friend what was going on. Until, that is, it was time for Clemmie to act.

'This will do nicely,' Clemmie said after the waiter had been and gone, leaving them with the menus to peruse.

'Are you sure they will sit at that table?' Prue checked, keeping her voice low, although there were only a few other diners in the restaurant so far and none of them were sitting close by. 'If they don't, I think I won't see them from here.'

'My husband is a man of habit and likes to sit at the same table in a restaurant and Caroline has seen him there,' Clemmie said assuredly. 'His predictability and love of the familiar is actually one of the things which I hope will make him reconsider. Destroying our marriage to be with Lavinia would bring a great deal of change to his life. He wouldn't like that at all.'

'Does *he* know what she wants? To end his marriage with you and marry her?' Prue asked. It was something they hadn't discussed before. 'I know you've heard about it from Lavinia's point of view, via Caroline, but does his Lordship know what his mistress is planning?'

'That's a question I don't yet know the answer to, but hope to very shortly... As you say, all I know comes from his mistress's point of view. She absolutely sees herself as the next Lady Campbell-Gryce,' Clemmie said quietly. 'He might not feel the same. If it wasn't for the fact that his latest mistress is Caroline's cousin's daughter, I wouldn't know much about it. Caroline's cousin is a terrible social climber and is so delighted that her daughter is being apparently courted by someone like my husband she is prepared to blatantly ignore the fact that Anthony is already married. She sees her daughter in my place and can't help crowing about how things are going to Caroline. Fortunately, she has no idea that Caroline and I are such good friends. Now, what shall we have to eat?' Clemmie picked up her menu and scanned down it.

Prue did the same, wondering if her nerves would allow her to eat anything at all.

'They're here!' Prue hissed, putting down her fork as she spotted Lord Campbell-Gryce and a stunning young woman who couldn't have been any older than her mid-twenties walk into the dining room arm in arm, following the maître-d to the table by the window as expected.

'I want to turn around and look,' Clemmie said, her fingers gripping the pristine white tablecloth. 'But I mustn't. Tell me what you see.'

'They're sitting down, he's facing towards us. I can only see her back, the waiter's hovering with menus. No, wait... the waiter's being sent away by his Lordship. Now they're holding hands across the table.' Prue glanced at Clemmie whose mouth was pressed into a thin line. 'Do you want to leave?' she asked seriously.

'Certainly not!' she snapped. Then, 'I'm sorry.' She gave Prue an apologetic smile. 'It's just...' She gestured with her hand. 'It's hard. Harder than I thought it would be.'

'Of course it is. Let's continue eating and I'll keep a watch and only tell you anything important.'

'You're right. Otherwise I'm going to drive myself crazy and be tempted to storm across there before the right time.' Clemmie picked up her knife and fork.

Over the next half an hour while they finished their main course then chose puddings and ate them, Prue kept a close watch on what their target couple were doing. It was clear that Lavinia was besotted with his Lordship. She had the mannerisms of a preening bird, Prue thought, flicking at her carefully coiffured shoulder-length hair, emitting a shrill, delighted laugh at things he said.

Throughout their meal, Lavinia frequently reached across the table and patted his Lordship's hand. As to whether his Lordship felt the same, Prue couldn't be sure. The devoted attention of a beautiful young woman was no doubt flattering to him.

'She's getting up,' Prue hissed as they were halfway through their coffee. 'She's taking her handbag. Looks like she might be heading to the ladies' room.'

'Right, this is it!' Clemmie sat rigidly in her chair for a few moments, taking a couple of steadying breaths. 'Watch carefully what happens.' She took the white napkin off her lap and stood up.

Prue reached out and squeezed Clemmie's hand briefly. 'Good luck.'

Their eyes met and Clemmie gave her a brief nod. Then, with her shoulders back and her chin up, she walked around the potted palms and over to where her husband sat.

Prue watched, feeling a shiver run through her at her friend's bravery. She was seeing Lady Campbell-Gryce in a new light. She was *formidable*, Prue thought admiringly, as she sat forward in her chair, her heart racing.

As Clemmie approached the table, his Lordship briefly looked her way then ignored her, clearly not recognising his wife, and when Clemmie sat down in the seat opposite him, which had been recently vacated by Lavinia, Prue saw him frown irritably and open his mouth, presumably to object to a strange woman seating herself unwelcomed at his table.

Then Prue saw the colour literally drain from his face, his mouth falling open into an O shape.

From where she sat, Prue couldn't hear what was being said. She was only able to watch how they both reacted to one another. It was obvious that his Lordship was caught out and flustered, folding his arms defensively across his chest, while

Clemmie leaned towards him, her finger pointing at him several times as she spoke.

Clemmie was still at the table and talking when Prue spotted Lavinia returning from the ladies' room. The young woman's forehead creased at the sight of a strange woman talking to his Lordship, sitting in the chair she'd vacated, but she still approached, holding her chin high. From her behaviour, Prue didn't think Lavinia had recognised Clemmie yet.

Clemmie and his Lordship both looked up at Lavinia's approach and to the astonishment of Prue and most of the other diners in the restaurant, which was now full, Lord Campbell-Gryce leapt to his feet, loudly knocking over his chair. Then he grabbed hold of the young woman's elbow and rapidly and almost violently steered her out of the restaurant, the white napkin from his lap fluttering to the floor as he went.

Like a white flag of surrender, Prue thought, and hoped she was right.

'What happened?' Prue asked when Clemmie returned and sat down, her cheeks pink and her eyes brilliantly bright.

'He was caught out and for once in his life couldn't come up with an excuse. I've told him what Lavinia wants and pointed out what he stands to lose,' Clemmie said.

The two women met each other's gaze and Clemmie took a deep, steadying breath, letting it out slowly though her pursed lips. 'I was glad to have you here,' she told Prue. 'I was right – I needed someone's support. I'll be for ever grateful to you.'

'You did wonderfully,' Prue told her, 'you were so strong.'

'You know, just between you and me, I wasn't feeling very strong at all. More like a feather about to be blown away in the slightest breeze.'

'And that's real bravery,' Prue said.

Just then the waiter arrived and topped up their coffee.

'Did you find out if he wants to marry her?' Prue probed when they were alone again.

'That I cannot tell you.' Clemmie took a sip of her coffee. 'I think he was shocked about what she wants. I don't think it was part of the plan when he got involved with her. So we'll see how he reacts. He knows two things for sure now: he's been caught red-handed and I am not going down without a fight.'

'His face! When he recognised who you were!' Prue said. 'He had no idea you were here – it was a total surprise.'

'He's felt very safe doing what he likes far from home but now he knows he's accountable for his actions wherever he does them. I must wait and see what happens, what he decides.' Clemmie smothered a yawn. 'I do apologise. I've suddenly come over so tired. Do you mind if we go back to Caroline's?'

'Of course not. We've finished our meal – which was lovely, at least what I could eat. I was so nervous! All the waiting and worrying you've been through has been exhausting for you.'

Clemmie signalled for the bill to be brought and quickly paid it.

'Thank you for being with me tonight. I'm not sure I would have been brave enough to do it otherwise – if bravery really is the right word. I was hardly facing down enemy guns…'

'Come on,' Prue said with a smile and, as they both stood up ready to leave, she hoped that the outcome of tonight would be what Clemmie wanted. Her friend had exposed her husband's adultery and deception and now all she could do was wait to see if it was enough to save Clemmie's marriage, family and home.

CHAPTER 20

'It's for you, Marianne,' Thea announced as she came back into the sitting room after answering the telephone.

Marianne stopped hand sewing the hem of the curtain for Evie's new home. 'Who is it?'

'Alex's sister, Marguerite.'

Marianne's heart sank. She'd been hoping that her sister-in-law might never telephone again.

Thea's eyes met Marianne's, a look of concern on her face. 'Do want me to tell her you're not available to talk at the moment?'

'No, I'd better get it over with.' Marianne stood up and placed the curtain on her chair.

Hettie, who like Marianne, Thea and Flo had gathered in the sitting room for the evening, put down her knitting and reached out and took hold of Marianne's hand. 'If Marguerite's still set on visiting you and the girls, we'll be with you. We won't let anything happen to you or them.'

'Thanks, Hettie.' Marianne gave the older woman a grateful smile before heading out into the hall, closing the sitting room door softly behind her. After taking a moment to prepare herself, she picked up the telephone receiver from where Thea had left it lying on the little table in the hall.

'Hello, Marguerite.'

'Marianne! How lovely to speak to you again!' Marguerite's plummy voice was upbeat. 'I've got some time off and wondered if it would be convenient for me to come and see you, and meet Emily and Bea, tomorrow afternoon? I've looked at the train timetables and I could arrive in Great Plumstead at half past one, then leave on the quarter to five train back to Norwich and my connection to the coast. Do say yes. I've had such a hectic few weeks and I've been dying for a chance to come and see you. Is tomorrow good? It's a Saturday of course, please tell me you aren't already too busy?'

Marianne had to make a quick decision. If she put Marguerite off this time, then she would try again, and the worry of when that might be would hang over Marianne. Perhaps it was better to get it over and done with, find out what was going on and if her mother-in-law was making another attempt to take the children.

'Yes, that sounds fine. We'll meet you at the station and walk you back to Rookery House,' Marianne suggested.

'That's jolly kind of you. I'm so excited about seeing you all and where you live. There's a queue forming for the telephone as usual so I must go. I'll see you tomorrow. Bye for now!' Marguerite rang off.

Marianne slowly replaced the receiver. She desperately hoped Alex's sister's visit wasn't to upset things. But she wouldn't be alone dealing with whatever might happen, Marianne reminded herself. She had good friends to support her if she needed them. Doing her best not to worry, she headed back to the sitting room to break the news of tomorrow's visit to the others.

CHAPTER 21

'Ma!'

Prue spun around, her face breaking into a beaming smile as she saw Alice hurrying towards her. The sight of her daughter wearing her smart blue WAAF uniform made Prue's breath catch in her throat. Even though it was more than a year since Alice had joined up, she still wasn't used to seeing Alice wearing it.

'Hello!' Prue wrapped her arms around Alice the moment she came within reach and held her tightly. 'It's so good to see you.' She finally released her daughter. 'You look so smart, grown up and responsible.'

Alice laughed. 'Our sergeant keeps a close eye on us, checks our hair is above our collars.' She patted the nape of her neck, where her long blonde hair was neatly rolled up to regulation length. 'And that our shoes are gleaming – the works!'

'Rather different from working for your Aunt Thea,' Prue said.

'Yes, muddy dungarees were more like it then. I do miss

Rookery House and everyone there, but I'm enjoying my job and living with the other girls.'

'I'm glad to hear that. Now, are you going to show me around York?' Prue slipped her arm through Alice's.

'Of course, shall we start with this beauty?' Alice looked up. From their meeting spot in Precentor's Court they were overlooked by the twin towers at the west end of the Minster.

'I'd love to,' Prue said. 'It's different to Norwich's cathedral, no huge soaring spire, but I like the more squareness of its towers. It sits as if it's watching over the surrounding city.'

'It's a landmark the pilots watch out for coming back to Elvington,' Alice said. 'When they see the Minster, they know they're nearly home.'

Prue had looked out for RAF Elvington, where Alice was stationed, from the train as they'd approached York. She knew it was sited a few miles to the south-east of the city but she hadn't been able to see it, though she had spotted a couple of planes coming into land, perhaps doing some circuits and bumps practising as they did at RAF Great Plumstead from time to time.

'The Minster must be a most welcome sight for those pilots, after what must always be very dangerous missions,' Prue said as they made their way to the cathedral's west door.

Stepping into the cooler interior, Prue was immediately struck by how the hustle and bustle of the city fell away behind them, replaced by a calm peace that seemed to soar up to the high arched ceiling.

'It's beautiful.' Prue found herself whispering, not wanting to disturb the tranquillity.

Alice spoke softly too. 'I love coming in here. Makes the war seem far away for a bit. Come on, there's something special I want to show you.'

As they walked arm in arm down the length of the

cathedral, Prue found her eyes drawn this way and that as she admired the beautiful interior. It made the inside of St Andrew's Church, back in Great Plumstead, seem very small and plain in comparison.

Alice steered them off to the left, through a smaller passageway and then an arched doorway into an octagon-shaped room.

'This is my absolute favourite place – it's the Chapter House.' Alice let go of Prue's arm and walked over to the far side of the room, crossing the beautiful floor with its mosaic patterns.

Prue gazed around her, slowly turning on the spot as she admired the many-arched stained-glass window panels around the walls and the beautiful ceiling. Her eye caught the stone carvings of heads and animals around the sides and she stepped nearer to have a closer look, noticing that each one was different.

'What do you think? Do you like it?' Alice asked quietly.

Prue turned around expecting to see her daughter standing close by but was shocked to see Alice on the far side of the room, a wide smile on her face.

'The shape of the room carries noise,' Alice said, continuing to talk quietly. 'Say something to me.'

'It's beautiful in here, I can see why you like it so much,' Prue said. 'Did you hear me?'

Alice laughed. 'I did. There's no secret whispering going on in here – everyone can hear what's being said!'

∽

Sitting in Betty's cafe, giving her feet a welcome rest after walking miles around York, Prue was eking out every precious moment she had left with her daughter. Alice was due to catch the lorry returning to RAF Elvington at five o'clock sharp, which was in just half an hour's time. Their day together had flown by and Prue had thoroughly enjoyed exploring York together.

'I have this for you.' Prue took something from her handbag and passed it across the table.

'What is it?' Alice asked, opening the piece of paper and reading it.

'It's Caroline's address, where I've been staying in Bootham Terrace. She's such a lovely, warm woman and she's invited you to visit and even stay if you have a short pass and can't get back to Great Plumstead for a visit in the time you have. She wants you to consider her place a sort of home away from home, the same as I do back in Great Plumstead for Waafs who get stationed at RAF Great Plumstead. I was telling Caroline about that and she said she'd like to do the same for you, and for any other Waafs who might need her help.'

'Thank you, I'd like that. Even if I don't have to stay there it would be nice to visit her. And I'll let my friends know too that we can all have a kindly home from home here if we need it!' Alice folded the piece of paper and put it in the pocket of her WAAF tunic. 'Sometimes I forget what it's like to live in a normal house, eat somewhere other than the cookhouse alongside so many other people. It's easy to become sort of institutionalised, living the ways and rules of the RAF. So I'll definitely get in touch with Caroline. Please pass on my thanks to her.'

'I will, and it's good for me too,' Prue admitted, 'knowing you have someone like Caroline to visit close by.'

Prue might only have known Caroline for a few days but the pair of them had got on like old friends, their WVS work giving them a shared interest and plenty to talk about. Prue had even gone with Caroline yesterday to help with her WVS work and it had been good to see what the women in York were doing. Prue would be taking away a few ideas of things they could try out back in Norfolk.

Alice glanced at her watch. 'I'm going to have to go, Ma. I mustn't miss the lorry going back or I'll be late and end up in trouble.'

'Shall I walk with you to where you're meeting the lorry?' Prue offered.

'I'd rather you didn't. It's hard enough to say goodbye as it is. Best to do it here.' Alice gestured towards the table where the tea things were set out. 'Stay and have another cup – there's still enough in the pot I think.'

Prue nodded. As much as she wanted to be with Alice for every second she could, she knew her daughter was right. 'Thank you for showing me around York. I've enjoyed it and seeing you has been wonderful.'

They stood up and she held Alice in a tight embrace. 'Look after yourself and I hope we can see each other again soon.'

'And you, Ma.' As Alice stepped back, Prue glimpsed tears in her daughter's eyes, which she quickly blinked away. With a final watery smile, Alice turned and left the cafe, weaving her way through the tables and out of the door.

Prue watched her go, her own eyes misting. Then she saw Alice waving at her through the window as she passed by and smiled. She was so proud of the young woman Alice had grown into, having the courage to leave home and do a responsible job as part of the war effort.

Picking up the teapot, Prue poured out a last cup, hoping that it wouldn't be too long before she shared a pot of tea with Alice again.

CHAPTER 22

Glancing up and down Great Plumstead station's empty platform, Marianne felt both tired and apprehensive about this afternoon. Despite her attempts not to worry about what might be the real reason behind Marguerite's visit, she hadn't been able to stop the questions she couldn't yet answer from going round and round in her head. She'd spent a restless night, her sleep broken and woefully limited leaving her feeling far from her best today, which was unfortunate and frustrating because she was sure she was going to need all her wits about her.

The one good thing that had come out of Marianne's wakeful night was that she'd had time to realise it would be wiser to meet her sister-in-law here at the station on her own, rather than bringing the girls with her, and so she'd left Emily and Bea in Hettie's safe hands back at Rookery House. Marianne had decided it was best to find out what was going on *before* she took her sister-in-law home. If it was the case that Marguerite was coming here under instruction from her and Alex's mother, then it would be better if she didn't get as far as Rookery House at all – or even saw the children. It would save any upset or emotional scenes and keep Emily and Bea well out of it.

Waiting for the train to arrive from Norwich, Marianne was awash with nerves. But in the way any mother lion would protect her cubs, she was determined to do whatever was necessary to keep her girls safe.

By the time the train came steaming into the station five minutes late, Marianne felt ready. She watched as the carriage doors opened and passengers climbed out, some of them villagers, others men and women members of the RAF dressed in their smoky blue uniforms. Standing out amongst those was one member of the Wrens in her uniform of navy blue.

Marianne waved to Marguerite and walked towards her, pasting a smile on her face.

'Marianne! How lovely to see you.' Her sister-in-law returned her smile and took hold of both of Marianne's hands, leaning forward to kiss Marianne's cheek. 'It's been so long since we last met.' She looked thoughtful for a moment. 'Golly, how many years? It must be nearly *four* years, before the war started, when you worked at Dorothy Abrahams making your amazing designs. And here we are, you now married to Alex with two little girls and me serving in the Wrens.'

Outcomes neither of them could have ever imagined back then, Marianne thought. None of Alex's family would have envisaged he would marry someone like her – a working-class girl with no family left and only her skills as a dress designer and maker to keep a roof over her head.

When they had first met, Marianne had been the girl in the background doing the fitting, the sewing and altering of garments for far richer girls like Marguerite and her friends who came to the designers to have dresses specially made for them. The gulf between Marianne as a worker, skilled though she might be, and Marguerite had been a wide one. Now to be greeted as Alex's wife by Marguerite felt strange and unsettling.

'Are the children here?' Marguerite looked around. 'I'm so much looking forward to meeting them.'

'No, they're back at Rookery House. I wanted to talk to you on my own first,' Marianne said.

'Of course, we can get to know each other as we walk to your home.' Marguerite put her arm through Marianne's. 'We never did chatter much when I had my dress fittings did we?'

Marianne shook her head. It wasn't the done thing. Her boss Dorothy Abrahams would have given Marianne short shrift if she'd tried to engage the clients in conversation beyond politely asking them to move this way and that as they were measured, or querying if the garment felt too tight or loose. Besides, very few of the clients had shown any interest in Marianne as a person. They were more interested in themselves or talking to whoever had come with them to the shop.

'No, we didn't chat much,' Marianne agreed. 'Let's sit down for minute or two here and talk.' She gestured towards a bench at the side of the platform, near one of the tubs that before the war would have been filled with flowers; it was now used for growing vegetables and showed signs of fresh shoots already sprouting from rich-looking soil.

'What is it you want to talk about?' Marguerite joined Marianne on the bench, seeming to sense Marianne had something important to say. 'It's not Alex, is it? Has anything happened to him?'

'No, he's fine as far as I know.' Marianne's heart was beating faster now that she was moments away from discovering the truth about this visit. 'What I want to ask you is, what are your intentions coming here?'

Marguerite looked confused. 'I'm sorry?'

'Your reasons,' Marianne persisted

'I – sorry, Marianne, I don't think I understand you. Are you asking why I chose to use my day off to come here and not–'

Marianne interrupted her. 'I need to know if you've come here today to help your mother try to take my children away from me.'

Marguerite's brown eyes, which were so like Alex's, widened dramatically. 'Oh! Goodness me! Of course not! Why would you think that?'

'Because after Alex was posted as Missing In Action your mother came to see me at Rookery House. She'd already decided that Alex was dead and she intended to take charge of Emily, and Bea once she was born. She wanted to remove them from me, take them to the family home and bring them up in a way fitting for Alex's children. Educate them in an appropriate way too,' Marianne explained, doing her best to keep her voice steady, though she could hear it wavering and she felt her whole body shaking. 'She was so threatening and I was terrified by what she was planning to do. Thankfully Alex turned up alive and in a POW camp, so she didn't carry out her threat. But I'm frightened she might still try again. Either in person – or through you.'

Marguerite closed her eyes for a moment. When she opened them again, they were awash with tears. She shifted so that she was sitting facing Marianne. 'I am so terribly sorry that my mother did that. It's *appalling*! And so insensitive to you, especially at such a worrying time and while you were expecting too. I had no idea she'd done that.' She placed her hand on Marianne's arm, her gaze meeting Marianne's and holding it. 'I promise you that I'm not visiting on her behalf and would *never* do such a thing even if she asked. She doesn't even know I'm here. I've come to see *you*, get to know you better and to meet my nieces, that's all.' She put her free hand on the front of her tunic over her heart. 'I promise.'

Marianne looked the young woman straight in the eye, searching for any sign of falseness, but she could only see what appeared to be genuine truth. She believed her. A wave of relief flooded through Marianne. 'I've been so worried.' Her voice cracked and she sobbed.

'Oh, darling Marianne, I'm so sorry if I've caused you worry. You are Alex's wife, my sister-in-law and mother to my nieces – I hate the idea of upsetting you. Alex adores you and I want us to become friends. Do you think we could?'

'Will you tell your mother about your visit?'

'Not if you'd rather I didn't. To be honest we don't speak very often or write either. She doesn't approve of me being a Wren and was furious when I came home and said I'd joined up. I won't say anything about my visit; just keep it between us.' Marguerite paused for a moment, her head slightly to one side. 'When my mother said she would take the children away from you, did she say what she planned to do with them?'

'She was going to get your and Alex's old nanny out of retirement to care for them.'

Marguerite scoffed. 'I can't imagine how awful Nanny would be now. She was dreadful to us and grew grumpier with every year that passed. Alex and I both hated her. If it hadn't been for the sweet and kind nursery maid who helped care for us, then our lives would have been entirely horrible. I would not have wanted my nieces to be under Nanny's charge. I wouldn't have stood for it!'

'Alex told me about her. There was no way I was going to let my girls be looked after by that woman.' Marianne let out a soft sigh. 'It's good to know you wouldn't have stood for it either. Now shall we go? I haven't told Emily that you're coming yet, just in case…'

'In case I was here on a covert mission for my mother?' Marguerite sighed. 'Now that you've told me what she did, I can quite understand your quizzing me. You did the right thing. You were defending your children.'

Marianne was growing to like her sister-in-law. Maybe she, like her brother Alex, was far better than the system that produced them.

'I was quite ready to bundle you back on the next train to Norwich with a flea in your ear and a warning to never return!' Marianne told her.

Marguerite giggled. 'You know, I think you would have put up a jolly good fight against my mother if things had turned out the worst about Alex. You wouldn't have let her take your girls away. And I would have supported you. We'd have made a fierce team.'

'Come on then.' Marianne stood up. 'Let's take you home to Rookery House.'

Marguerite sprang to her feet. 'I can't wait! Thank you for believing in me. I won't let you down, you know. My brother's important to me and so are you and your girls. You're family to me, Marianne. A good part of it too, much kinder and caring than my own parents.' She put her arm through Marianne's. 'I'm so excited to see where you live and meet everyone.'

As Marianne walked out of the station, arm in arm with Marguerite, her heart felt a lot lighter than it had when she'd arrived earlier. Her questions had been answered and the potential threat from Alex's mother could be dismissed. She herself might, of course, come back again and interfere, but if her mother-in-law did that, Marianne now knew she'd have Marguerite as a powerful ally to support her.

~

Marguerite passed Hettie's approval, the older woman being on hand as she'd promised Marianne, and the afternoon flew by. As the time approached for Marguerite to leave Rookery House to return to the station, Marianne's initial doubts about her sister-in-law's visit had been firmly quashed. It was clear that Marguerite was genuine in her wish to spend time with them and get to know them. Her delight at meeting and being with Emily and Bea shone through and her warm, caring nature towards them had endeared her to the two little girls. Alex would be pleased to hear how well his sister and daughters had got on.

'Are you sure you don't want us to walk you back to the station?' Marianne asked. 'It's no trouble.'

'I'll be fine and you already have plenty to do without me adding to it. It's been such a wonderful afternoon. Thank you so much for allowing me to come and visit.' Marguerite's eyes met Marianne's, a silent message passing between them in recognition of what they'd discussed at the station. 'I'm so lucky to be an aunt to these two delightful girls.' She addressed this to Bea who was seated on Marguerite's lap fiddling with the shiny brass buttons on the front of her tunic, and Emily, who'd snuggled in beside Marguerite on the sofa while she'd read a book to them and didn't seem keen to change her position.

'We hope you'll come and visit us again,' Marianne said. 'You're welcome any time.'

Marguerite beamed at her. 'I'd like that very much. I don't

know how long I'll be posted in Great Yarmouth but while I'm there I will make the most of being close by. I'd invite you to come and see me but it's much safer here for you with Yarmouth being in the thick of things sometimes.' She glanced at her watch. 'As much as I would love to stay here with you all, I really must go.' She put her arms around Emily and Bea and gave them a loving cuddle. 'You two take care and try not to grow too much until the next time I see you!'

'Hettie says we grow quick like weeds,' Emily said as Marguerite let go of them, stood up and gently placed Bea on the sofa beside her sister.

Marguerite laughed. 'But you are both so much nicer than weeds.' She turned to Marianne and embraced her. 'You and Alex have the most wonderful girls. I'm lucky to have you as my sister-in-law.' She stepped back and, keeping her hands on Marianne's arms, said, 'We must keep in touch; will you write to me please?'

'I'd be glad to,' Marianne agreed.

Gathering up her Wrens' hat from where she'd left it on the table, Marguerite put it on, ready to leave. Marianne picked up Bea and with Emily taking her aunt's hand they went out of the house and around to the front gate.

'Goodbye then,' Marguerite said, kissing each of them on the cheek. 'Take care and I hope I'll see you all again soon.'

'Bye bye,' Emily said waving, which Bea copied.

'You're welcome here any time,' Marianne said again, genuinely hoping her sister-in-law would return. This afternoon had been a revelation, she thought as the young Wren set off towards the village, turning round to return their waves for one last time before she disappeared around the bend. As Marianne had started to properly get to know Marguerite, the young woman had proven to be a kind, thoughtful and caring person. Thankfully she was nothing like her domineering, snobbish mother but instead showed the same warm and caring traits as Alex. Marianne was glad to have her become part of their family and, with Alex still a POW for who knew however long, having his sister come and visit could prove to be a real bonus.

CHAPTER 23

It was Sunday afternoon, the second day of May, and Evie was on her afternoon break from her shift at the hospital. She'd changed out of her uniform into her borrowed dungarees and come over to the old grooms' rooms to meet Ned. Now he'd finished painting all the rooms it was time for them to put the furniture in place.

'Where shall we put the table?' Ned asked. 'There,' he pointed to the middle of the room, 'or over to the side by the wall?'

Evie stood, her hands on her hips, trying to decide. 'Let's try it in both places and see.'

Together they moved the wooden table to the centre of the kitchen and Evie circled it. 'Umm, I'm not sure if this would work – it makes it harder to move around. I suppose with it just being the two of us eating at it most of the time then it makes sense to put it against the wall. We can always pull it out into the middle when we have guests.'

They moved the table to the side of the room. 'That's better,' Ned agreed. He took two of the four chairs they'd got from the attic and tucked one at each end of the table. 'There, perfect. We can put the other two either side of the window.' He moved them into position.

Item by item they worked around the room, moving the cupboard that would store their pots, pans and crockery into place, and another one for their food stuffs. Evie unrolled one of the rugs and placed it in front of the sink. 'To keep our feet warmer while we're washing up.'

With the kitchen in some order, and just the crockery and pans to be unpacked into the cupboards, they headed upstairs, each of them carrying a couple of drawers from the chest of drawers to make it lighter when they took the main body of it up.

'Where are we going to put the beds?' Evie asked as they went into what was to be their bedroom.

'Against that wall facing the window. That way we'll get the morning light coming in,' Ned suggested. 'Let's bring the frames up next and tie them together.'

As Evie helped Ned carry a bed frame up the stairs she was relieved they only had one flight to climb, unlike the four flights the men had carried it down, negotiating dog-leg bends on the way.

'Just as well they're only single frames. I'm not so sure I could have managed a double,' Evie commented as they put the frame down in the bedroom and she rubbed her arm where the metal footboard had pressed into it as she'd carried it.

'They're sturdy enough.' Ned gave the frame a shake. 'Come on, one more to go.' He put his arm around her shoulders. 'Then we need to work out the best way to tie the frames securely together. We don't want them separating and us landing in a heap on the floor in the middle of the night.'

Evie laughed. 'Certainly not!'

After they'd brought up the second frame, Evie left Ned to fetch the two mattresses and sort out the bed frames while she returned to the kitchen, telling him to call for her help if he got in a tangle.

As she unpacked the mixed assortment of crockery, placing it neatly in the cupboard, a memory of the grand dinner service that she and Douglas used to eat off flashed into her mind. It had been a wedding gift from his godmother and Evie had never liked it, but Douglas had. He would have been appalled at the prospect of eating off the mixed assortment of plates that she was unpacking. They were the remnants left over from sets used in the Hall by staff over the years, some plain blue or white, others with patterns of small sprigs of flowers on. Nothing fancy, but good serviceable crockery which she and Ned were grateful to have. Nothing about this new home, from its former use as accommodation for grooms, to its second- or third-hand furniture and kitchen goods, was anything like the smart flat she and Douglas had shared in London. It might have had expensive furniture, thick rugs and fancy curtains, but it had lacked what was most important in a home – happiness.

'Evie!' Ned's voice called from upstairs. 'Can you come up? I am going to need you after all.'

Glad to leave the memory of her previous married home behind, Evie headed upstairs to find Ned lying on his side on the bed. He patted the mattress beside him. 'Come and see if holds together with both of us on it.'

Evie joined him on the bed, lying next to him, then snuggling up as he put his arm around her. 'So far so good,' Evie commented.

Ned's eyes met hers and he smiled before kissing her.

Evie kissed him back, but as much as she would have liked to remain where they were, she wriggled free of his arms. 'It's very tempting to stay here but I'm due back on duty in...' She checked Ned's watch, her own being pinned to her uniform which was back in the staff changing room at the hospital, 'only fifteen minutes. I know Matron's on leave for a few days, but it wouldn't do to be late – someone would notice.'

'I know,' Ned groaned. 'But soon you won't have to rush off. It's going to make such a difference to us, Evie. Our own home, *together*.'

She stroked his cheek. 'I know. Now let's get the last bit of furniture for the bedroom carried upstairs before I go back. I'll polish everything next week when we move in. I've run out of time today.'

Reluctantly, Evie and Ned got up and brought the body of the chest of drawers upstairs and pushed it into place by the wall in their bedroom.

'Two rugs are for in here too, one on either side of our bed. I hate putting my feet on a cold floor in the morning.' Evie gave a mock shudder.

'I didn't know that.'

'We have lots to learn about each other.' Evie gave him a wry smile.

'I'm looking forward to learning,' Ned said.

Evie grabbed hold of his hand and looked at Ned's watch again. 'I must go as I need to change back into my uniform.'

'I'll finish unpacking in the kitchen and bring those rugs up for the bed. Don't want your feet getting cold.'

Evie gave him a kiss. 'You, Ned Blythe, are the best of all men.'

With that, she dashed out of the room and ran down the stairs, hearing Ned's warm laughter as she went, her heart full of love for him.

CHAPTER 24

Back at home after her trip to York, Prue had returned to the routine of her busy life and was spending the afternoon sewing in the workroom. Gloria was the only other person there and the pair of them chatted easily as they sewed.

'I 'ad a letter from Charlie arrive yesterday,' Gloria said. ''e was docked in New York for a few hours and posted it there. Said 'e'd love to show me the sights there one day. Imagine! Me in New York!' Gloria gave a throaty laugh, keeping it quieter than usual so as not to wake her daughter, Dora, who was having a nap. The little girl lay sleeping on some cushions on the floor, near the shelves on the far side of the room.

Prue glanced at her friend, whose upbeat words thinly veiled the worry she felt for her husband. Charlie was a merchant seaman working on one of the ships that ploughed back and forth across the Atlantic bringing precious goods to the country. Each crossing carried the danger of his ship being attacked and potentially sunk by enemy submarines.

'I'm sure you would love it there – and that New Yorkers would love you!' Prue said, turning the handle of the sewing machine she was working at. 'I hope you get to visit one day. Any news on when Charlie will have some leave and come and see you?'

'No. But then Charlie likes to surprise me with a visit, doesn't he? Says it's more fun that way. Remember 'ow 'e turned up my first Christmas 'ere. What a wonderful surprise! Each time 'e's done it since has been just as good.' Gloria gave a wistful sigh. 'Let's 'ope it ain't too long before 'e turns up again.'

'I hope so too,' Prue agreed as she held the material for the pair of boy's trousers she was making, guiding it under the sewing machine's bobbing needle. She recalled her first meeting with Gloria's husband that Christmas at Rookery House. He was a great bear of a man who exuded good cheer and friendliness and who clearly adored Gloria. Any time they could snatch together was always a happy occasion. Their marriage was the opposite of what Prue's had been.

'How's Alice?' Gloria asked, deftly hand stitching the hem of a skirt.

'Very well,' Prue said. 'I think being in the WAAF suits her. She likes being stationed near York and gave me a lovely tour of the city. I think it did us both good to be together. I was...' She halted at a loud *rat-a-tat-tat* of the front door knocker.

'Shall I get that?' Gloria stood up. 'Easier for me to leave what I'm doing than for you when you're machining. Might be one of the other women come to sew. Though they usually just give a quick knock and let themselves in.'

'Yes, please, I'm coming up to a tricky bit and don't want to stop.' Prue kept on sewing, listening to the sound of her friend's high-heeled shoes as they tip-tapped along the hall to the front door. With the whirring of the sewing machine, Prue couldn't properly make out the voice of the caller or even tell if it was a man or a woman. She pressed on with her work, carefully guiding the fabric under the needle, keeping the seam width even, thinking she'd find out soon enough who was calling.

'Prue?' Gloria returned to the workroom, closing the door into the hall behind her. 'You've got a visitor.' She lowered her voice, leaning closer. 'It's a man and 'e looks like Victor. Says 'e's your...'

Prue let go of the sewing machine handle, her stomach twisting. 'Brother-in-law? Claude?'

Gloria nodded, her face concerned. 'I asked 'im to wait outside.' She put a hand on Prue's shoulder. 'Are you all right? I didn't like the look of 'im if I'm 'onest.'

Prue let out a sigh and, keeping her voice low, replied, 'Well not really... he's...' She waved her hand in the air. 'Put it like this, I hoped I'd seen the last of him.' Was he back to have another go at claiming part of Victor's business, as he'd tried to last year? Prue thought he probably was.

'Do you want me to tell 'im it ain't convenient right now? To sling 'is hook?'

'He'll only come back again. No, I'll deal with him.' Prue stood up.

'Shall I come with you? I'm good with difficult men. Look at Percy Blake – 'e treats me with the utmost respect now after I told 'im what's what.'

Prue gave a laugh. 'I'm glad you're here and I'll be sure to give you a shout if I need you, but don't worry, I can handle Claude.'

After taking a moment to compose herself and straighten her apron, Prue marched out into the hallway, ready to do battle if necessary. And there she found, to her annoyance, that Claude hadn't done as Gloria had asked and waited outside. Instead, he was standing just inside the front door with a small bunch of daffodils wrapped in newspaper held clumsily in one hand. Spotting her, he pushed the door closed behind him, the catch slotting into place with a loud *clunk*, and advanced towards her.

For the briefest of moments Prue had the unpleasant sensation that Victor was back as the two brothers looked so similar – same build, hair and eye colour. But this wasn't Victor, Prue sharply reminded herself. Her husband was dead and buried in the village churchyard. She'd witnessed his lifeless body being brought out of the ruins of his mistress's home in Norwich last year.

'Good morning, Prudence!' Claude removed his hat as he came to a halt in front of her. 'I've brought you some flowers.'

The use of her full name irritated Prue – it had only ever been used by Victor and Claude.

She fixed her eyes on Claude's, which were the same icy blue as Victor's had been. 'Claude. This is a surprise, what brings you here today?'

'I thought I'd come and visit.' He held out the flowers for her to take.

Ignoring them, Prue asked, 'Why?'

Her coolness didn't seem to register with Claude. 'It's been a year since we lost Victor. I thought I should come and see how you were managing. If you need any help at all.'

'I'm managing perfectly well.'

Claude's eyes drifted towards the door of the workroom which stood ajar. 'Can I… I'd just like to have a look…'

Before she could say anything, Claude had side-stepped her, pushed open the door of the workroom and gone inside.

Suddenly Prue heard a strange, high-pitched yelp which was closely followed by the sound of Dora bursting into tears, no doubt woken by the odd sound.

Prue hurried into the room and saw Gloria had picked up her daughter and was cradling the little girl in her arms.

Dora's face was turned away from Claude as she was soothed on her mother's shoulder.

'What have you done?!' Claude asked, rounding on Prue, his voice shrill and out of control. 'This room is *Victor's study*!'

'*Was*,' Prue said. 'Victor doesn't need it any more so it's been repurposed and made into a workroom for sewing, knitting and mending as part of the war effort. For the use of the women of this village, open to all.'

'But… but…' Claude stammered, his face turning puce.

'But what?' Prue said, putting her hands on her hips and raising her chin.

'Well I was hoping to…' Claude was flustered, his eyes flickering about the room. Prue could almost see his mind working overtime. He blinked rapidly, but when he spoke, he'd managed to make his voice softer and accompany it with a strained smile. 'You're right of course Prudence. These days no space can be left idle. What you're doing is most admirable. Very public spirited of you.'

Behind Claude, Prue saw Gloria looking daggers at him and their eyes met briefly. They could both see Claude for what he was. He might sweeten his words, but his character was all too plainly revealed.

'I wanted to give you these.' Claude held out the small bunch of flowers to Prue again, an obsequious smile on his face.

Prue reluctantly took them, thinking that it might speed things along to him leaving. Gloria's features had darkened. Prue wondered what her friend might have said and done, if she hadn't had Dora to soothe.

'I must get back to work,' Prue said shortly.

'Ah, yes. Very good. I can see how busy you are and since you have people here…' He glanced towards Gloria and Dora briefly… 'I'll leave you to it. I can let myself out. Goodbye,

Prudence.' He gave a quick bob of his head and scuttled from the room. Moments later the front door opened then closed with a satisfying *clunk*.

Prue let out a loud sigh of relief.

'What on earth was all that about?' Gloria asked, gently swaying from side to side as she rocked her daughter back to sleep. 'I'm sorry to be so direct, Prue, but 'as 'e been courting you?'

Prue shuddered. 'I sincerely hope not! Not if he was the last man on earth would I *ever* consider being with a man like him. Victor was bad enough; I have no plans to enter a relationship with his brother!'

'Fair enough and I'm glad to hear you say it. He's a wrong'un, as they say in these parts.'

'You're picking up our Norfolk sayings very well,' Prue observed with a smile. 'Claude is indeed a wrong'un. Just like his brother.'

''e did seem mighty put out about the workroom though,' Gloria mused.

'I'm not sure why it would bother him so much. My affairs and what I choose to do aren't any of his business. He hardly ever even came to the house. Though I suppose when he did, they'd end up in the study, talking,' Prue said. 'Maybe he thought I would keep Victor's study as a shrine to his memory.'

'That's a thought. *Something* set 'im off – 'e didn't half let out a yelp when 'e came in 'ere. You should 'ave seen 'is face. But it's better 'ow it's being used now, a room for everyone.' Gloria crouched down and lay the sleeping Dora back on the cushions, covering her with the blanket.

'I wondered at that sound he made!' Prue said, her eyes wide. 'My first thought was that *you'd* done something to him!

Then I came in and saw you were holding Dora, so that put my mind at rest.'

Gloria winked at her. 'I'm not slow to defend myself or my friends. But you're quite right, 'e saw the room and let out a noise like a cornered cat and that woke Dora. She won't want to see *his* angry face again, I can tell you – and neither do I!'

'Me either,' Prue said ruefully. 'Now, how about some tea? And I'll put these flowers in the kitchen. Daffodils are my favourite. I couldn't throw them out. They're a sign of the hopes of spring and they're beautiful – and that's nothing to do with who brought them.'

As Prue made her way into the kitchen, she couldn't shake off the feeling that Claude would be back. That she *would* have to see him again. Whatever he'd come for he hadn't been able to say or do, whether it was because Gloria and Dora were there, or due to his shock at seeing Victor's study so utterly changed. From her experience of Claude, Prue knew that if he wanted something he wasn't quick to give up. Much as it pained her to think it, Prue knew that whatever reason had compelled him here to see her, it would inevitably do so again.

CHAPTER 25

There was a good turnout for tonight's event, Hettie thought, making her way along the aisle separating the rows of chairs towards the front of the village hall. The sound of chatter, punctuated with bursts of laughter from members of Great Plumstead's Women's Institute as they settled themselves into their seats, had hardly diminished since Prue had called for them to sit down ready to start. But then these meetings were an opportunity for friends to catch up who might not have seen each other since the last time the WI put something on.

Glancing to her left, Hettie caught the eye of Beattie Southgate and saw that her Land Girl Iris was with her. The pair of them smiled at Hettie, mouthing 'Hello'. She returned their greeting, glad to see that they'd come along again. Hettie had encouraged them to join as it was a chance for both women to get to know more people, plus have a night out away from the farm.

Reaching the end of the aisle, Hettie headed for her seat between Flo and Marianne, who were sitting in the front row. Just then she noticed the outside door open and five young

Waafs come in and slip into the empty chairs nearer the back of the hall. Hettie gave them a wave before sitting down, thinking she must speak to them in the tea break.

'Elspeth and Marge have just arrived,' Hettie said quietly to Flo. 'I'm glad they still come to our meetings.'

'I...' Flo began but fell silent as Prue got to her feet from where she was seated behind the long table facing the hall, flanked by rest of the WI committee.

'Good evening, everyone! It's lovely to see you all here again. Welcome to our new members and our guests. Tonight, we have a speaker, Mrs Arbuthnot.' Prue gestured towards a woman sitting in the front row but on the other side of the aisle from Hettie, next to Gloria. 'Mrs Arbuthnot is here to speak to us about how we can make the best of our clothes coupons by making the most of what we have in ingenious ways. Please give our speaker a warm welcome.'

Prue clapped and the rest of the women joined in as Mrs Arbuthnot took her place in front of them, ready to begin her talk.

Hettie listened as the speaker told them about how to reuse things, like a blanket, an old felt hat or pieces of carpet to make slippers. When the examples Mrs Arbuthnot had brought were passed around the audience, Hettie had a good look at them. The simple message of the talk was the necessity to think creatively, to make what you needed from what you already had or could get. Doing that saved precious clothing coupons.

'Some clever ideas there,' Marianne said to Hettie as the women clapped at the end of the talk. 'Things we can do for the clothing depot to add more to what we loan out to people.'

Hettie nodded. 'There's an old felt hat in my wardrobe that's seen better days but it would be ideal for slippers. Perhaps I should have a go at making some, but...' She gave her friend a smile. 'I may need to ask your advice, as you're the expert sewer, not me!'

'I'd be happy to help,' Marianne said.

'Time for our break!' Prue called out and the hall erupted into more chatter. There was a scraping of chairs as the WI members and guests got up and headed for the table near the kitchen doorway, where tea things had been set up ready.

'Come on, let's get a drink.' Hettie stood up and joined the surge of women, eager for some refreshment.

'It's a happy stroke of luck that we're all benefiting from,' Elspeth was saying, her Scottish accent soft and lilting. 'Being able to push the tables back in the cookhouse and have a wee dance on a Saturday night without having to leave the aerodrome has been great.'

Hettie was pleased to hear that the young Waafs were finding ways to let their hair down. Dancing the night away to a newly formed band on the aerodrome was perfect for them, after their long days of hard work.

'That all sounds a lot of fun,' she said. 'I always enjoyed dancing when I was your age – and I still do now when the fancy takes me.' Hettie chuckled.

'Maybe we should suggest to Prue that we have a dance in the social part of these meetings,' Marge said. 'Someone could bring along a gramophone and some records.'

'Ask her,' Hettie urged. 'Music always goes down really well. Our games of musical chairs and musical bumps are often the funniest and most enjoyable activities!'

The Waafs giggled. 'We love playing musical chairs. Let's hope there's a game of it tonight.'

'I'm not sure what Prue's got planned for us next,' said Hettie, 'but I've offered to do the washing up so I'd better go and get on with it. The sooner it gets done, the sooner I can join in the fun and games.' She gave the girls a wink and, after collecting their empty cups, carried them along with her own over to the trolley.

'Can we make a start again!' Prue called out.

While the rest of the women returned to their seats, ready for the business part of the meeting, followed by the social half hour, Hettie pushed the trolley of empty teacups into the kitchen. She was joined by Ted's sister Hilda, who was another long-standing member of the village WI.

'Do you want to dry while I wash?' Hilda asked.

'I don't mind,' Hettie said as they tipped out the dregs and stacked the cups on the side. 'This lot won't take us long.'

As they worked side by side, their talk turned to the subject of Ada.

'I've never seen her at a meeting,' Hilda said. 'Is she not interested?'

'I have tried to convince her to try it because I think she might enjoy it, but Ada is Ada!' Hettie raised her eyebrows. 'My sister won't be shifted once she's decided something and she must have made up her mind at some point that WI meetings aren't for her.'

Hilda nodded. 'Is she happy working at the Hall?'

'Oh yes.' Hettie chuckled. 'It suits her very well and I'm glad for her because it was a heavy blow losing her home the way she did. To have it pulled down to make way for the aerodrome after living there for so long wasn't easy. But she's bounced back and is the same old bossy Ada.'

'You don't let her boss you around now, do you?' Hilda asked, putting another washed cup on the draining board.

'Of course not! But she still tries. When she came to see me last week, I told her about going to the pictures with Ted. She was most put out about it, didn't think it right.'

Hilda's eyes widened. 'What's the problem with that?'

'Nothing. Ted and I both had a lovely time.' Hettie placed the cup she'd dried on the table alongside the others, ready to be put away when they'd finished. 'But Ada was worried about what people might think, seeing us together. She thinks they could get the wrong idea about me and Ted.'

Hilda shook her head. 'Well, some people have got nothing better to do than talk about things they know nothing about and don't concern them. I think it's smashing the way you and my brother have become good friends, after all these years. It has done Ted the world of good and helped him settle into the village again. Of course...' Hilda's eyes met Hettie's as she paused her work, 'if it ever *did* become something more than friends, you would both have my blessing, Hettie. I want you to know that.'

'Thank you, Hilda,' Hettie replied, 'though just being good friends is enough for me. Ted's good company and we get along fine as things are. I don't think either of us wants anything more.'

'He's a fine man,' Hilda said, resuming the washing up.

'He is,' Hettie agreed. She was pleased to have Hilda's support and understanding.

A rise in the level of noise coming from the hall signalled the end of the business part of the meeting.

'Sounds like the fun and games are about to begin,' Hettie said. 'Five more cups to go and we can put this lot away and join in.'

'Come on then, let's get a move on – I don't want to miss out!'

CHAPTER 26

Evie woke on her last morning at Rookery House at the sound of the soft snick of the bedroom door closing. She glanced over to see that Flo's bed was empty, the top sheet, blankets and patchwork quilt thrown back after she'd got up. She must have gone down to the bathroom to get washed.

Lying against her pillow, Evie let out a gentle sigh and revelled in being able to lie in bed for longer. She was thankful that this morning the ringing of her alarm clock hadn't shattered her sleep at a twenty past six, as it did most days, giving her sufficient time to prepare for her shift at the hospital. But there was no need for that today, as it was her day off and the day that she'd be moving into her new home with Ned. Today's move was stirring a mixture of emotions in Evie – happiness and excitement but also some sadness too that her time here living with her friends was ending. Today was going to be bittersweet.

As Evie cast her eyes over the room, she recalled how it had felt like a haven to her when she'd first moved in back in the autumn of 1940. Newly arrived from London, escaping her past and her abusive marriage, Rookery House had been a place of refuge where she could start again with no one knowing her. Slowly, the warmth and welcome of the people living here had broken down the shell she'd built up around herself and she had made true lifelong friends who were more like family.

Ned's arrival as a blind patient at the hospital had threatened Evie's new-found security. He'd known her in her past life, when he'd worked as chauffeur to her parents-in-law. She remembered how terrified she had been, worrying that if he regained his sight, he would expose the truth about her. How strange life can be, Evie thought, how the threads that weave it can twist and turn in unexpected ways. Here she was about to move into her new home with Ned – the man who she'd once feared would shatter her new life. But he hadn't. He had only added to it, making it even better. Evie was grateful for how things had turned out.

The bedroom door opened and Flo came in wearing her dressing gown over her nightdress.

'Morning! I hope I didn't wake you. I tried to be as quiet as I could.'

'No, I woke up after you'd gone.'

Flo sat down on the side of her bed, facing Evie. 'Today's the day. How are you feeling?'

'Happy *and* sad.' Evie looked at her friend. 'It feels bittersweet.'

'I understand,' Flo sounded sympathetic. 'I'm going to miss you and our chats in here.'

'I'll miss you too, but I hope we will see each other often and chat. It won't be across the width of the rag rug while we lie in our beds – but we will make time to meet and do things together,' Evie reassured her, recalling the many heartfelt talks they'd shared, both confiding secrets with each other. Their discussions had helped Evie and she always appreciated Flo's understanding and advice and had returned the favour to her friend.

'When are you leaving?' Flo asked.

'Ned's coming at midday to help me carry my belongings. So I need to be ready by then.'

Evie hadn't yet packed anything, wanting to stretch out her time here and keep things looking normal for as long as she could, with no suitcases or boxes standing in the corner of their bedroom ready to go.

'I'll pack after breakfast.'

'Talking of which.' Flo placed a hand on her stomach, as it gave a loud rumble. 'I'm hungry!' She stood up. 'I've loved sharing a room with you, Evie. Thank you.'

'Likewise.' Evie reached out her hand and Flo took hold of it.

'I'm thrilled for you and Ned. You are the loveliest couple and you both deserve a long and joy-filled life together.'

'Thank you.' Evie gave Flo's hand a gentle squeeze before letting go of it and throwing back her covers. 'It is time I got up as it's going to be a busy day.' She grabbed her dressing gown, which was draped over the footboard of the black iron bedstead. 'I'm off to the bathroom.'

∼

After her last breakfast at Rookery House, when the children had been full of excitement about Evie and Ned moving into their new home, Evie made her way upstairs to begin her packing. She took her two suitcases from under her bed and placed them on top of the colourful patchwork quilt.

She opened the largest case and filled it with her clothes, removing them from the chest of drawers that she shared with

A JOYFUL SPRINGTIME AT ROOKERY HOUSE

Flo. Every garment Evie owned, except for her nurse's greatcoat, would fit into it. That hadn't always been so, she thought. There had been a time when she would have needed several large suitcases and hat boxes to accommodate all her outfits. But not now.

When she'd arrived at Rookery House, it was with just one case containing her nurse uniforms, some basic clothes and the certificates of her nursing qualifications. In escaping from her life with Douglas, she'd not been able to bring much with her, needing it to look like she'd just gone out for the day before being killed in an air raid. If she'd taken too many of her belongings, it could have looked suspicious. She'd had to leave all her precious books.

Evie glanced at the bookcase with her collection of books that stood on the far side of the room. It had been a monumental day when she'd returned to the flat she had once shared with Douglas to retrieve them. By then he'd been killed in Africa and she knew it was safe to go there. She remembered how she'd packed them into a case padded out with her woollen jumpers to protect them while she carried them home on the train to Rookery House. Today her books would be going with her on another journey. She didn't need to leave them behind this time.

There was a gentle knock on the door.

'Come in,' Evie called.

The door opened and Hettie stepped inside, a colourful bundle of patchwork folded in her arms. 'How are you getting on?'

'Good. Everything will fit in my suitcases.'

'Including all your books?' Hettie asked, eyeing the bookcase. 'You've bought quite a few since you came here, along with those you fetched from London.'

'I hope so.'

'If not I've got an empty cardboard box from Barker's Grocer's downstairs for you to use.'

'A box is easier to pack books in. Thank you, Hettie.'

'I've got something else for you, but you don't have to take it if you'd rather not. I won't be offended.' Hettie shook out the bundle she was holding, a waterfall of gloriously coloured patchwork quilt pooling down to the floor.

Evie gasped. 'It's beautiful.'

'It's big enough to fit a double bed but I've never had need of it so it hasn't been used. I bought it from one of the maids at the Hall who used to make them. It's such wonderful work I couldn't resist it. She made those too.' She nodded to the quilts covering Evie and Flo's beds.

'Are you sure you want to give it away? It's so gorgeous.' Evie touched the quilt, noticing how finely it was sown.

Hettie nodded. 'Yes, it's been folded up in a drawer in my room and it's too lovely not to be seen and enjoyed. I'd be delighted if you and Ned would have it for your new home with my love and all good wishes for your life together.'

Evie's eyes filled with tears and she threw her arms around the older woman, embracing her tightly. 'Thank you so much. We will treasure it and it will look so cheery and colourful in our bedroom.'

Hettie hugged her back, and when they stepped apart, Evie saw her friend's eyes were shimmering with tears that emphasised their blueness behind her round glasses.

'Good.' Hettie gave her a warm smile. 'I'll take it downstairs, ready for when Ned comes. Now, are you going to manage to take everything? You've got your cases, a box if you pack your books in there, your bicycle and I've got some food for you to take to set you up to start with.'

'That's so kind of you, Hettie.'

'I thought with you being back at the hospital tomorrow

and working long shifts, it won't be so easy for you to get to the shops.'

'That's something Ned and I need to work out, but we'll soon sort it. As for how we're going to carry my things up to the Hall…' Evie grinned. 'Ned says he's going to bring a wheelbarrow. I'm not sure if he was joking — or not!'

~

Evie was ready and waiting by the bay window in the sitting room, when Ned turned in at Rookery House's gateway at midday, pushing a wheelbarrow. Evie laughed out loud, thinking that with the number of things they had to carry, including the beautiful quilt Hettie had given her and the box of provisions, it was exactly what they needed. She waved, and spotting her, Ned grinned at her, then headed around to the back of the house.

Dashing out of the sitting room and into the kitchen where she'd left her cases, box of books and everything else ready to take, she saw everyone had gathered there – Hettie, Thea, Flo and Marianne and her two daughters.

'Here she is,' Hettie said. 'Has Ned arrived?'

'Just coming round.' As Evie spoke, she saw him walk past the window. 'And with a wheelbarrow!'

Hettie's eyes widened. 'So he wasn't joking.'

'No!' Evie laughed as she headed out the door to greet Ned.

'Hello.' Ned took hold of her hands in his. 'Are you all set?'

Evie nodded and kissed him. 'I'm ready to go to our new home.' Saying those words brought tears to her eyes and Ned pulled her into his arms and held her tight. 'It's a big day for us,' he said softly, his lips in her hair.

She held on to him for a few moments more before releasing him. 'I didn't think you were really going to turn up with a wheelbarrow.' She gestured at the barrow, which was lined with hessian sacks to cushion the ride for her luggage.

He grinned. 'What better way for a gardener to transport his wife's belongings to their new home?'

Hettie appeared in the doorway. 'Will you stop and have something to eat with us, Ned?'

'I wish I could, but I've got to get back to work. Mr White's been good about me having time off to bring furniture down from the attic and to move Evie in today. It wouldn't do to take advantage.'

'Fair enough. In that case, I've made you both up some sandwiches to have when you get there,' Hettie said.

'You're a treasure, Hettie,' Ned said appreciatively. 'Right, now we'd better load up.'

With help from Thea and Flo, it didn't take long to carry Evie's belongings outside. They stowed the suitcases in the wheelbarrow along with the box of books, and with her greatcoat folded up on top.

Evie had already collected her bicycle from the shed, leaving it leaning against the scullery wall. She placed the folded patchwork quilt Hettie had given her in the basket at the front. She would hang the two shopping baskets filled with their picnic, plus enough provisions to set them up for a few days, from the handlebars as she set off.

'Mustn't forget this.' Hettie took a ration book out of her apron pocket. 'You'll need this now.' She held it out to Evie.

'I'd forgotten about that, thank you.' Evie put it in her handbag. 'Well, that's everything, I think.'

'You're not far away if you've left anything behind.' Thea stepped forwards and held out her arms. 'It's been a pleasure having you living here. You will always be welcome at Rookery House.'

Evie stepped into her embrace. 'Thank you for everything. I'll never forget your kindness to me.'

More hugs followed as one by one, Evie said farewell to her friends. Even little Emily and Bea gave her legs a tight squeeze. By the end, Evie's eyes were swimming with tears.

'Go on.' Hettie squeezed Evie's hand. 'Ned and your new home are waiting for you.'

'Thank you, all of you.' Evie's voice wavered with emotion and she did her best to smile. Turning away, she walked over to her bicycle, fighting to regain her composure. Taking the weight of her bicycle by leaning it against her body, she threaded the handle of a basket over each handlebar, placing them so they balanced each other. Then with a deep breath, she turned and pushed the bike towards where Ned was waiting with the loaded wheelbarrow.

His eyes met hers, a silent message passing between them as he checked she was all right. She nodded.

'Goodbye and thank you,' Evie said, giving her friends a wave. 'I'll see you soon.'

With calls of 'Good luck' and enthusiastic clapping from the children, Evie and Ned headed off to their new home together.

～

'This is delicious,' Ned said after his first mouthful of sandwich.

'It's an unusual combination, but it works well,' Evie agreed, taking another bite of her own sandwich, its herby cream cheese and beetroot filling oozing out from thick slices of Hettie's homemade bread.

'Our first meal in our new home,' Ned said after he'd

finished. He glanced at his watch. 'I'm going to have to go back to work. Will you be all right?'

'Of course! I have plenty of unpacking to do and I need to polish the furniture. I didn't have time to do it on Sunday. Then there are curtains to hang.'

'I feel bad leaving you to do it on your own.'

'You shouldn't. You've done loads of work getting this place ready, far more than me. Now it's my turn.' They both stood up and Ned wrapped his arms about her and hugged her before giving her a kiss. 'I'll see you later.'

Left on her own, Evie sat down at the table again to eat the last of her sandwich. As she ate, she gazed around the room, which had been utterly transformed from when she'd first seen it. The cobwebs and layers of grime had gone, the walls had been given a fresh coat of white paint and, with the furniture carefully chosen and retrieved from the Hall attic, it had been turned into a homely place. It just needed the curtains putting up and the provisions placing in the cupboard to make it complete. Then Evie could move on to unpacking her cases and adding her books to the bookcase in the sitting room upstairs. They would join Ned's books, which he'd moved in with the rest of his things over the past few days.

Evie quickly finished her lunch. There was no time to waste – she had work to do.

Evie had saved sorting her books out till last. She'd hung the curtains that Marianne had shortened for her, polished the wooden furniture with the beeswax and lavender polish Hettie had given her and now it was time to unpack her precious books.

Perching on an armchair, Evie opened the box she'd

brought from Rookery House and took out the first book – it was *Persuasion* by Jane Austen. She smiled to herself, recalling the day she'd bought it at the book shop in Wykeham. She'd been there with Ned. It was before they'd become a couple and were on an outing as friends. He'd collected *The Keys to the Kingdom* by A. J. Cronin that he'd ordered.

Evie scanned Ned's books already on the bookshelf, found *The Keys to the Kingdom* and placed her copy of *Persuasion* next to it.

It had been their mutual love of books and reading that had first brought her and Ned together, when he'd been a patient here at the hospital. With his eyes hidden behind bandages, Evie had read to him and they'd talked about books they loved, comparing opinions and thoughts on the stories they both knew. Their friendship had grown from there, developed into love and look where it had brought them now, Evie thought. A marriage – of sorts. Sharing a home. And, importantly, much happiness.

Evie let out a sigh of contentment and unpacked the rest of her books, mingling them amongst Ned's. By the time she'd finished, the bookcase was three quarters full. There was still room to add more and grow their library. Perhaps on her next weekend off they might take a trip to Wykeham and visit the book shop and add to their collection. Evie would suggest it to Ned when he got home later.

CHAPTER 27

It was Friday afternoon and Hettie was experimenting. She'd mixed up a different batch of scones to her usual recipe and was eager to find out how it turned out. Going by the delicious smell as they'd cooked, they would hopefully taste good, thought Hettie as she picked up the pan holder. Opening the oven door in the range, she stooped to take out the baking tray, her glasses fogging with condensation from the rising heat, but she'd seen enough to know that they were ready. Golden on top and nicely risen.

Hettie put the scones on a rack on the table to cool and, while she waited, made a start on washing up the mixing bowl and rolling pin she'd used to make them. With her hands in the hot soapy water in the sink, a memory from her childhood flashed into her mind. There she was, like now, waiting for a bake to cool that she had made with her mother, the pair of them washing up. The recollection was a precious one, as her mother had died when Hettie was only eight years old.

It had been her mother who'd first taught Hettie how to bake, inspiring her love of cooking, which had eventually led her into her job as a cook. Hettie still carried that love with her and would cook till the end of her days. It was as much a part of her being as the stars were of the night.

'Afternoon, Hettie!'

The man's voice made her jump. She'd been so absorbed in her memory and thoughts that she hadn't realised the back door had opened.

'Hello, Ted.' Hettie beckoned him in with a soapy hand. 'You're just in time to be my first tester.' She nodded her head towards the scones cooling on the kitchen table.

'Happy to oblige.' He stepped inside and closed the door behind him. 'They smell delicious.'

'It's an experimental recipe.' Hettie dried her hands on the tea towel. 'I've got some fresh cream cheese to go with them.'

After fetching the cream cheese from the pantry and taking plates from one of the dressers and a knife from the drawer in the table, Hettie cut two scones in half, then spread each of them with a liberal helping of the white cheese, which like the scones was speckled with small dark green pieces.

'Give me your honest opinion.' Hettie passed Ted a plate with a scone on.

'Thank you. It looks good. What are the green bits?' Ted asked as he picked up a half of scone.

'I'm not telling you... yet!' Hettie said. 'I want to see what you think, how well the flavour has come through.'

Ted bit into the scone, a curious look on his face. After he'd swallowed his mouthful he smiled at Hettie. 'Delicious! Wild garlic?'

Hettie nodded. 'Yes, not too strong?'

'Definitely not, enough to give the flavour, but not overpowering. Try it for yourself.'

Hettie bit into her scone and chewed, letting the combined flavours of the crumbly scone, cool creamy cheese and wild garlic dance across her taste buds. 'Ummm.' She nodded to Ted, watching as he polished off the second half of his scone.

'I'm pleased with that,' Hettie said after finishing her mouthful. 'Would you like another one?'

Ted grinned. 'Oh, yes, please. It's a bit late for wild garlic. Isn't it past it's best now?'

'Yes,' Hettie said, spreading cream cheese on a second scone for Ted. 'I harvested some earlier to dry so I could use it for longer. This is the first time I've used some of the dried leaves and it has worked well.' She passed the scone to Ted. 'Did you come to see Thea?'

'No, I came to see you. I'm going to Norwich next week and wondered if you'd like to come with me? Make a day of it. I remember you saying it's a long time since you last went.'

'It is.' Hettie paused, thinking through what she had planned for the coming week. 'What day are you going?'

'Any, what would suit you?'

'How about Thursday? It's not my turn at the WI market stall in Wykeham and I'm not on duty at The Mother's Day Club.'

'Thursday it is then. I'll look forward to it.'

'So will I.' Hettie returned his smile.

CHAPTER 28

Apple blossom was one of the many delights of spring, Marianne thought, gazing around at the froth of pink and white petals adorning the trees in Rookery House's orchard. The blossom had attracted a host of bees, their gentle hum filling the air as they worked.

Marianne reached up for a nearby branch and pulled it down to admire the clustered flowers, each one beautiful with white, pink-tinged petals surrounding golden yellow stamens at their heart. She leaned closer and inhaled the delicate scent.

She had come out for a walk around Rookery House's garden on her own while her daughters were having their afternoon nap. Hettie and Flo were in the house and had offered to keep an ear out for the girls if they woke, but they should sleep for a good hour. Time on her own was most welcome – it gave Marianne the chance to think. On a day like this, under a beautiful blue sky the colour of forget-me-nots, it was a joy to be outside and she'd been drawn here to the orchard now the trees were in flower.

No matter what was going on out in the world, the seasons

kept on turning, Marianne thought. The fruit trees came into bud and flowered and the bees pollinated them. Tiny apples formed, grew over the summer and were harvested in the autumn. Then the leaves fell and winter held everything in waiting until the entire cycle started once more. Such familiar certainties were soothing in what was otherwise an uncertain world, especially now with the war on and no sign of an end to it yet.

'You look thoughtful.'

The voice made Marianne start and she turned her head to see Thea walking towards her, wearing her bee-keepers hat and veil.

'I didn't know you were out here,' Marianne said.

'I've just been checking the hives.' Thea waved her hand towards where the beehives stood at the far end of the orchard, out of sight of where they were. 'All's well and the bees are busy foraging.' She glanced up at the trees, watching as the insects flew from flower to flower. 'I love the sound of the bees at work in the blossom.'

'So do I. It's a soothing background noise. Very calming.'

'It is,' Thea agreed. 'I rarely see you out here on your own though – you usually have Emily and Bea with you.'

'They're both having a nap. As it's such a lovely day, I thought I'd get outside on my own for a bit. I wanted to have a think. When I saw the blossom I just had to come and have a closer look.'

'Are you all right?' A look of concern passed over Thea's face.

'Yes, I'm fine, but I wish there was more I could do to help Alex. I know I already send him next-of-kin parcels as often as I'm allowed and write to him every week, but it doesn't seem enough.' Marianne frowned. 'He tells me in his letters that he's doing well and is enjoying studying civil engineering. He wants to sit exams and get some qualifications for after the war, thinking it might be useful. Lots of the men are using the time to study. That's all good, but...' She twisted her mouth to the side. 'I just feel that there *must* be more I can do.'

'It sounds like you're already doing all you can for Alex,' Thea reassured her. 'But the Red Cross always needs more funds to keep on sending out food parcels to POWs and supplying them with books for their studies and so on. How about organising an event to raise money for the Red Cross' Prisoner of War Fund? My friend Violet's ambulance station in London put on a concert to raise funds for them. I remember Violet telling me in a letter how they held auditions for different acts – they had singers, comedians and some of her crew even did a sketch playing characters from the *ITMA* wireless programme and set it in their ambulance station!' Thea smiled. 'The concert was a great success and they all had a wonderful evening. The idea to hold it came from Bella, who's one of the ambulance crew, wanting to raise money for the fund because her brother was a POW in Italy.'

'It sounds marvellous, but I don't think I could organise something as big as a concert,' Marianne said. 'I wouldn't know where to start and I don't have the time, with the girls to look after.'

'A concert is a lot to sort out, I agree, but perhaps there's something else that could be done and more fitting for a village event, something others could help with. Why not ask your friends at The Mother's Day Club?' Thea suggested. 'Between all of you, you're bound to come up with some good ideas.'

Marianne nodded. 'I will, thank you.'

'And once you have a plan, I'll help as much as I can. Knowing this village, you won't be short of other people willing to pitch in either,' Thea reminded her. 'Now, I've promised George and Betty that we'll go for a walk in the wood this afternoon to see the bluebells, so I'll leave you in peace.'

Left on her own again, Marianne considered what her friend had said. She would talk to the other women at The Mother's Day Club next week and see what ideas they could come up with between them. If they raised money for the Red Cross, then it would not only go towards helping Alex but many other POWs too.

CHAPTER 29

Prue wheeled the trolley loaded up with tea things out of the village hall kitchen. It had been a busy morning at The Mother's Day Club mending clothes for the clothing depot and darning another batch of airmen's holey socks from RAF Great Plumstead. Everyone was ready for a break.

'I ain't 'arf glad to see the tea trolley. I'm parched!' Gloria said as Prue approached the table where the women were sitting, the garments they were mending spread out in front of them.

'We've made good progress again this morning,' Prue said, filling a cup from the large urn and handing it to Gloria, who passed it on.

'Mornings like this and extra time in the workroom at your place 'ave made an 'uge difference to what we can do,' Gloria said, passing another filled cup along. 'But there's always more to be done! More 'oles to darn.' She let out a throaty chuckle. 'Keeps us out of mischief!'

'While we're having a break, I want to ask for your help,' Marianne said from her seat opposite Gloria.

Prue turned her attention to the young woman who was a stalwart member of The Mother's Day Club and highly valued for her dressmaking expertise, which had been a great help with altering and making garments for their clothing depot. Everyone here had learned so much from Marianne, whose careful guidance meant their sewing skills were all vastly improved.

'What do you need help with?' Prue asked, pouring out the last cup of tea for herself and sitting down.

'I want to raise money for the Red Cross's Prisoner of War Fund and I'm not sure what to do,' Marianne explained. 'I was hoping you all might suggest some good ideas that would work well in Great Plumstead. Thea told me about a concert her friend helped organise at her ambulance station in London. But I'm not sure a fund raising concert would work here.'

'We could 'old a dance 'ere in the village 'all,' Annie suggested.

'A raffle.'

'Put on a play.'

'Have a fancy dress ball.'

Ideas came thick and fast and Prue saw Marianne listening to them all.

'Hang on a minute.' Prue put her hand up to quieten the group 'Those are all good ideas, but they wouldn't appeal to everyone in the village. In my experience, the more people in a community that are involved, the better the outcome and, in this case, hopefully the more money that would be raised. Perhaps we should think of something that would appeal to all ages.'

'The summer fete we 'ad the other year was good that way,' Gloria said. 'Our singing group sang there and there were races for the children and stalls. Everyone enjoyed themselves. I did!'

There were nods of agreement around the table.

'How about a May Fair?' Marianne suggested. 'Since the last one was a summer fete. I know they've been practising maypole dancing at the school, as George and Betty have been talking about it at home. Perhaps the children could dance at the fair.'

'I think a May Fair sounds like an excellent idea, but…' Prue's gaze met Marianne's. 'You would need help to organise it. It's far too big a thing to do on your own. I would be happy to work on it with you.'

'And me.' Gloria put her hand in the air.

Hands went up around the table – each and every woman was willing to give their time.

'My sister's 'usband 'as just become a POW in Germany,' Annie said. 'So many of us are friends or family of captured soldiers. We all want to support them the best we can and this is one way we can do that.'

Marianne smiled gratefully. 'Thank you, everyone. I couldn't do it on my own.'

Gloria reached across and took hold of Marianne's hand. 'You ain't ever alone with us lot to help you, ducks.'

'The first thing we should decide is when to hold it,' Prue said. 'It's the eleventh of May today so we don't have long to organise things if we want to have it this month.'

'It should be on a Saturday so more people can come,' Marianne said.

'Good idea,' Gloria agreed. '*Where* shall we 'old it? It would be lovely to 'ave it outside, on the village green, but there ain't no guarantee it won't be a rainy day.'

'We should check when the village hall is available and book it as a back-up in case the weather's bad – I'll have a look now to see when it's free.' Prue got up and fetched the hall bookings diary from where it was kept in a cupboard just inside the main door. 'Right,' she said, sitting down in her seat at the table again, opening the diary and flicking through to the pages for May. 'Looks like the only free Saturday this month is the twenty-second of May.'

'That makes our decision easy, then,' Gloria said. 'Saturday the twenty-second it is!'

Prue pencilled in the booking as the women drank their tea. 'That gives us...' She counted through the days in the diary from the day's date. 'Just ten days to organise a May Fair.'

Marianne frowned. 'Is that long enough?'

'It will 'ave to be!' Gloria said with a laugh. 'Don't worry, ducks, between us we can get everything done. The first thing to do, now we know when and where, accounting for all weathers, is what we're going to 'ave *at* the fair. Stalls and so on.'

'Maypole dancing,' Marianne said. 'It's a lovely thing to see and would bring parents and children to the fair. If it's a rainy day, perhaps they could dance in the school hall.'

'I can ask the headmaster when I meet my two boys from school this afternoon,' Annie offered.

Prue carefully tore a blank page out of the back of the village hall diary and started to write a list, adding maypole dancing at the top, along with Annie's name. 'We'll leave you to organise that, if that's all right?'

Annie nodded.

'What about stalls?' Prue asked.

Suggestions flew in, thick and fast, and Prue added them to the list, including those they'd had at the summer fete which had proven most popular.

'How about a second-hand stall?' Marianne suggested. 'I

could put posters up around the village asking for donations to sell.'

'Another good idea.' Prue wrote it on the list. 'I'm sure lots of people have things they don't want any more which we could sell. Shall I put you down to organise that?'

'Yes,' Marianne agreed. 'Where should donations be brought to?'

'Here, there's plenty of space and we can sort out what we get the Friday before the May Fair,' Prue said. 'It will be interesting to see what gets donated.'

By the end of their tea break, which lasted far longer than usual, Prue had a long list of stalls and various things that needed to be done to prepare for the fair. Many of the women had more than one thing to organise but everyone was upbeat about the challenge ahead of them. With just ten days to go, it was going to be busy fitting everything in alongside all their other commitments. But something Prue had learned about her friends at The Mother's Day Club was that when called upon to act they were an incredibly resourceful and motivated bunch of women who could be relied on to get things done.

CHAPTER 30

It was five days since she and Ned had moved into their new home and one of the many things Evie loved about it was how it had made her mornings a little slower. There was no need to set her alarm clock as early as she had while living at Rookery House and no bicycle ride through the darkness, wind or pouring rain before work, or after. Now all she had to do was walk across to the other side of the cobbled courtyard, Evie thought as she stirred the porridge in the saucepan that she was making for her and Ned's breakfast. It gave them time together before they each went their separate ways to work and with her working such long shifts it was especially precious.

'It's ready,' Evie called out to Ned, who was shaving in the scullery next to the kitchen. She removed the saucepan from the top of the stove and served the porridge into the two bowls that she'd set out ready on the table.

Ned came into the kitchen patting his freshly shaven, smooth cheeks with a towel. 'Perfect timing, thank you.' He kissed Evie and was about to sit in his place at the table, which faced the window, when he started, exclaiming, 'What on earth?!'

Before Evie could ask him what was wrong, he'd fled from the kitchen, then out of their front door, leaving it banging behind him.

'Ned?' Evie called after him. 'What's going on?' With the empty saucepan and wooden spoon still in her hand, she dashed over to the window and the sight that met her made her gasp, the saucepan and spoon falling from her hands and hitting the tiled floor as she hurried outside.

Evie ran across the cobbles, her heart beating hard against her ribs, to where Matron Reed, dressed ready for work in her uniform, lay slumped on the ground by the Hall's back door with Ned supporting her head. Matron's eyes were closed.

He looked up as Evie approached. 'I saw her fall. She was standing here by the door and then just slithered downwards, crumpling up.'

Evie crouched beside Matron and took hold of her wrist, feeling for her pulse, which was strong but beating faster than usual. The older woman's skin felt hot and Evie put her hand to her forehead. 'She's got a fever, no doubt about that.'

'Shall I pick her up?' Ned asked.

'I need to check there's no broken bones first.' Evie gently ran her hands along Matron's legs and arms but all seemed well.

Matron's eyes flickered open, a confused look on her face. 'I... I stepped out for some air,' she croaked.

'Do you hurt anywhere?' Evie asked.

'My head, my throat, everywhere,' Matron mumbled. 'Legs like lead.'

'We need to get you into bed and call the doctor,' Evie said kindly.

Matron didn't argue but gave a small nod of agreement.

'Ready to lift?' Evie put her arm under Matron's and around her back and nodded for Ned to do the same on her other side, the pair of them preparing to take the weight.

'One, two, three,' Evie counted. They pulled her up onto her feet, keeping her supported between them. Then Ned scooped Matron into his arms and followed Evie as she led the way in through the back door of the Hall and into the servants' quarters. 'Matron's room is up on the second floor; can you carry her up there?'

Ned nodded.

'The quickest way will be using the back stairs,' Evie said, heading for the servants' stairway. She appreciated Ned was strong from all his gardening work, but Matron was no lightweight and carrying her upstairs wouldn't be easy for him. The fact that her boss wasn't protesting at being carried, and not giving out orders, was an indicator of how ill she was, Evie thought as she motioned for Ned to go ahead of her so that she could follow and be there to help if he faltered.

Thankfully, Ned's strength held out. Arriving on the second floor, Evie hurried in front to Matron's bedroom, which was down the end of the corridor away from the rooms used as extra wards for patients when necessary. She hesitated outside the door, as this was a place she would never have dared enter before without permission, then chided herself because these were extraordinary circumstances and Matron was making no sign of objecting and in fact had her eyes closed, her head resting against Ned's shoulder.

Stepping inside the room, Evie was surprised at the burst of colour, from the cheerful patchwork quilt spread over the bed to the raspberry-pink dressing gown draped over an armchair. She would have expected Matron to prefer more muted colours but then she had never seen her boss wearing anything other than her uniform.

'Sit her here,' Evie said, indicating the armchair by the fireplace to Ned. Then she addressed her patient. 'I'll need to change you out of your uniform before you get in bed, Matron.'

Matron opened her eyes as Ned lowered her into the chair and she grabbed hold of his hand. 'Thank you,' she mumbled, her voice raspy.

He patted her arm. 'Glad to help.' Turning his attention to Evie, he asked, 'What else can I do?'

'Go downstairs and speak to the night staff nurse on duty. Tell her what's happened and to telephone for the doctor. I'll get Matron changed and into bed.' She put her hand on Ned's arm. 'Thank you.'

'Will you be all right?'

'Of course,' she reassured him. 'I'm doing my job and we have Matron in the best place for her.'

'If there's anything else I can do, send a message. I'm sure Mr White would be fine with me doing whatever I can if it's to help Matron.'

'I will. Tell the staff nurse I'll stay here till the doctor comes,' Evie said.

Once Ned had gone, she helped Matron out of her uniform and into her nightgown which Evie had found folded up under her pillow. Then, with her arm around Matron, Evie supported her across the room to her bed. The way Matron leaned heavily on her showed how weak she must feel, and she virtually collapsed on to the bed.

'There.' Evie tucked the sheet and blanket over Matron, who lay back against her feather pillows with a heavy sigh.

'I'll have a little rest and get up again and be back on duty.' Matron's usually strong and assertive voice was barely a whisper.

'I don't think you'll be going anywhere today,' Evie said gently.

'But the hospital… the patients…'

'Will all be fine. You've trained your staff well and we know the routines. Everything will run as normal. The important thing for you to do now is rest and get better.' Evie laid a hand on Matron's forehead, which was still burning. 'I'm going to fetch some tepid water and a cloth to make you more comfortable till the doctor comes.'

Matron gave a small nod and closed her eyes.

After fetching what she needed, Evie pulled up a wooden chair from the dressing table and sat by the bed. She dipped the cloth in the bowl of water, then dabbed it over Matron's flushed face to help cool her down. Whatever the older woman had was causing her temperature to rocket. No one else in the hospital had had anything like it. Matron must have caught it on her recent travels to see her sister in Cambridge; travelling there and back by train would have meant encountering many people on her journey.

It was the first time Evie had ever seen Matron ill. She always seemed to have the constitution of an ox, as the saying went. But suddenly she was very poorly and seeing such a normally strong woman so unwell was a shock. Despite their difficulties in the past, Evie was worried for her and desperate to do all she could to help.

～

'From the look of things, I think Matron has influenza or something similar,' Dr Shawbrook said after he'd carried out his examination. Evie and he had come out into the corridor, leaving the patient dozing in her bed. 'My concern is that it could infect patients on the wards.' He regarded Evie through his wire-framed spectacles. 'Matron must be nursed by one person alone to limit the spread of infection. Since you've already started caring for her, it should continue to be you, Nurse Blythe.'

Evie nodded, knowing that what he said made perfect sense. 'I should be on duty in the hospital today. If I'm up here, they'll be short-staffed.'

'Better that than the patients – and staff – becoming infected,' he warned her. 'I'll speak to the nurses and make sure they do all they can to help you, bringing up food and supplies so you don't have to go down. Naturally, you must take every precaution to avoid catching the influenza yourself. Wash your hands frequently, don't touch your face, wear an overall over your uniform when nursing Matron, keep her to a separate bathroom, ventilate the room with plenty of fresh air and so on. Make sure she takes plenty of fluids, carry on tepid bathing and steam inhalations as necessary. Hopefully within a few days she'll be over the worst.'

'I'll stay with her and look after her well.'

'Jolly good, and if Matron's condition deteriorates, then you send for me straight away.'

'I will.' Evie watched as he strode off down the corridor and then descended the main staircase. She hadn't been expecting anything like this to happen today, and it would not be just for one day either. It would be for as long as it took for Matron to start feeling better. Evie would do all she could to help her, putting her nursing skills into practise on what she suspected would be one of the most exacting patients she'd ever had!

She would need to get a message to Ned, tell him what was going on and ask him to send her some things as she'd be staying overnight here both to look after Matron and to prevent taking the infection home to him.

She let herself into Matron's room again and checked on her patient, who for now was sleeping peacefully.

∽

It was early evening and Evie's day had passed differently to her normal shifts at the hospital. With Matron as her sole patient, it had been quieter and less hurried. Evie had felt a twinge of guilt that her absence from the wards would have made more work for the nurses on duty but in the long run it was the sensible option. If the men became ill with whatever Matron had, then it might put them in danger and the health of their patients always came first. And if infection spread to the nursing staff, it would put running the hospital under serious strain. Evie was certain that being Matron's sole nurse was the right thing for her to do.

Throughout the day they had been kept well supplied with food and drinks, with loaded trays being delivered outside the door. Only Evie had eaten, as Matron hadn't wanted anything, but importantly she had taken plenty of drinks.

Sitting in the armchair from where she could monitor her patient, who was sleeping, Evie heard a gentle tapping on the door. Answering it, she found a basket had been left there. It contained her clothes, wash things and, to her delight, two books. She glanced along the corridor and saw Ned standing some yards away.

'How are you getting on? And how's Matron?' he asked in a low voice.

'She's asleep and no worse, thankfully. I'm taking good care of her,' Evie replied. 'Thanks for these and the books especially.' She gave him a grateful smile. 'I'm a lot less busy than during a usual shift so I'll have time to read while Matron's sleeping.'

'I thought you'd need something to read,' Ned said. 'I'll be reading too – I'll miss you tonight.'

'And I'll miss you. It's not what we expected, not even a week after moving into our home – me having to stay here overnight.'

'I know, but at least you're not far away.'

'Matron's window overlooks the kitchen garden,' Evie said. 'I saw you working out there today.'

'I'll look out for you then tomorrow. Wave to me.'

'I will. I'd better get back.' Evie blew Ned a kiss. 'Take care.'

He blew a kiss back to her. 'And you. I'll watch out for you looking out of the window.'

Back in Matron's room, Evie returned to the armchair, buoyed up by seeing Ned and his thoughtfulness at bringing her some books to read. She watched Matron sleeping for a few moments, glad to see that the older woman was resting. Her eyes then drifted to a framed photograph on the bedside stand. She'd looked at it several times today, wondering who the man in it was. Clearly it was someone important for Matron to keep his photograph close by her. It made her realise how little she knew about Matron's life before she'd come to Great Plumstead Hall Hospital. She didn't even know where she'd grown up, her soft Scottish accent the only clue. Matron Reed had kept her personal business private, carrying out her role running the wards and overseeing the care of the men. What lay behind the photograph, Evie wondered, what life had Matron lived and with who?

CHAPTER 31

'It's shocking to see it like this.' Hettie hung onto Ted's arm as she stared at the damage before them.

They'd come into Norwich on the train, arriving at City Station which bore the scars of the Baedeker raids. Then walking into the city centre they'd passed by the ruins of houses, or gaps where houses used to stand. Here in Rampant Horse Street, once familiar shops had gone, destroyed by enemy bombs.

'It's not until you see it with your own eyes that it really hits you. I'd heard about it from Thea and Prue, after they were here with the WVS canteen, but…' Hettie's voice wobbled and Ted patted her hand.

'Seeing it for yourself makes it real,' he said. 'This is only from a couple of nights of Blitz. Whatever must London be like after all those huge air raids they suffered?'

Hettie gave a shudder. 'This awful war. When will it end?' She let out a heavy sigh before lifting her chin. 'I'm sorry, Ted. We've come here on a lovely day out and there's me being all maudlin. We must carry on just as the good people of

Norwich are doing. We should be glad about what's left. The castle is still standing, the cathedral, the city and guild halls. It could be far worse.'

'What would you like to do?' Ted asked.

'How about we have a wander along and just see where that takes us?' Hettie suggested. 'Then stop for a bite to eat somewhere, just enjoy being in Norwich for the day.'

'Sounds a good idea to me,' Ted agreed.

∼

After they'd had a meal in a cafe, Hettie and Ted headed through the Tombland area with its quaint shops and restaurants, then towards the cathedral. Passing under an old stone arch leading into the cathedral grounds, Hettie stopped for a moment to stare up at the tall, sand-coloured spire thrusting up into the sky, contrasting beautifully against the azure blue, cloudless backdrop.

'What a magnificent sight!' she said. 'It doesn't matter how many times I've seen it before, it never fails to make my heart swell. Imagine building the cathedral way back hundreds of years ago, before they had all the advances we've got today.'

'It dwarves our church in Great Plumstead,' Ted said.

'And all the others in Norwich. All of them are special in their own unique way, but this is like the grandmother of all our Norfolk churches.'

They continued their walk, passing through Cathedral Close and heading down towards Pulls Ferry on the banks of the River Wensum, which snaked its way through the city.

'Can I ask you something?' Hettie glanced up at Ted.

'Of course. Is everything all right?'

'Yes, I think so. But I was wondering, do you worry about

us being seen out together? Not just here in Norwich, I mean, but in the village or in Wykeham where people know us.'

Ted halted, his face concerned as he looked at her. 'No, not at all. Has someone said something?'

'Ada. When I last saw her, I told her we'd been to the pictures and she was rather bothered about how it might look. What people will think and say about us.'

'What would they say?' Ted asked. 'There's no crime in going out to the pictures or on a day out to Norwich with a friend, is there?'

'No, of course not, but there are some who might gossip and make assumptions,' Hettie warned him. 'If they do then that's their problem, not mine. I enjoy your company very much and relish going out to places together. I just wanted to let you know what's been said to me and to make sure you won't be surprised or affected by it, should some busybody say anything to you.'

Ted took hold of one of Hettie's hands in both of his. 'You're my friend and I treasure that. We have wonderful talks and laugh a lot together. Visiting places with you is fun. I don't care what anyone else might think or say. As long as we're happy in each other's company, that's what matters.'

'Thank you,' Hettie said. 'I guessed that would be what you'd say, but I had to check what you thought,' she explained.

'My sister's very pleased that we're friends,' Ted reassured her. 'She thinks it's good for me.' He let go of Hettie's hand and offered her the crook of his arm. 'Shall we walk on, see if there are any swans on the river?'

Hettie put her arm through his. 'It would be my pleasure.'

As they continued towards Pulls Ferry, Hettie's heart was lighter, having checked what Ted thought and discovered that all was well. Their friendship had developed gradually, and unexpectedly, but had grown to be an important part of her life now. She very much enjoyed having someone to talk, laugh and share things with, outside of her wonderful friends at Rookery House.

Hettie couldn't help thinking that her overly bossy older sister might benefit from having a friend like Ted in her own life.

CHAPTER 32

'Will you be able to get everything done in time for tonight?' Thea asked as she brought the WVS canteen to a halt on the road outside Prue's house in Great Plumstead.

Prue turned towards her sister in the driver's seat. 'I hope so. There's been a lot of correspondence from the regional and national WI offices to sort through and it's my job as secretary to read it and report to the committee at our meetings. I'm just a little more behind than usual. You bringing me home is a big help. Saves me some time to spend on the pile of paperwork I need to wade through.'

'WVS, WI, The Mother's Day Club, Rural Pie Scheme, WI allotment alongside running a home. Plus helping organise the May Fair!' Thea counted each of them off on her fingers. 'You do a lot. Don't you ever think it's too much?'

'Sometimes,' Prue admitted. 'But usually I balance things out. It's only because the WI committee meeting's been moved forwards to today instead of next week that I've been thrown out of kilter. It will be fine, I'm sure.' Prue opened the cab door. 'Thanks for dropping me off.'

'Anytime. Now go and sort that pile of paperwork out.' Thea grinned. 'I'll see you soon.'

Prue climbed out and closed the door behind her. She waved as her sister drove off, heading for the WVS depot in Wykeham. Usually, they would both go at the end of their weekly canteen run and then get the train back to Great Plumstead together but this afternoon, with Prue needing to prepare for tonight's meeting at half past six, she needed every spare extra minute she could get.

Hurrying through the garden gate, she let herself in the front door, went through to the kitchen and banked up the stove, then put the casserole she had prepared earlier into the oven to cook for tea. She was about to go upstairs and change out of her WVS uniform before starting work on the WI papers when there was a sharp *rat-a-tat-tat* on the front door knocker. Prue hesitated, wondering if she should ignore it but knowing she couldn't – it might be important, maybe even a telegram with unwelcome news.

The moment she opened the door and saw who was standing there, Prue wished she'd made a different decision. It was Claude. He'd come back, just as she'd feared he would.

He removed his hat and gave her an oily smile. 'Good afternoon, Prudence.' He looked her up and down, taking in her green WVS uniform. 'You look very smart, I must say.'

'Afternoon Claude. I'm about to do some work to prepare for an important committee meeting tonight so I don't have the time to stop and talk.'

'I understand. What I've come to ask you won't take long. Do you mind if I come inside for a moment? I'd rather not say it on the doorstep.'

'Very well.' Prue stepped to the side and opened the door wider for him to step in, thinking if he was going to question her about Victor's old business then she'd rather he didn't do it on the doorstep either.

'It's been over a year since we lost Victor,' her unwelcome guest was saying, 'and enough time has passed to mourn him. Life must now go on.'

As Claude paused for a moment and she closed the door, Prue couldn't help thinking that she herself had never mourned for Victor because in truth his death had been a release. Would she ever mourn for him? She didn't think so. Victor was gone and she and their children were alive and thriving, and that was about that, as far as she was concerned.

What Claude said next brought Prue's attention back to the present so sharply she gave a little jolt, almost as if she'd been given an electric shock.

'And so my dear, the time has come for me to offer you my hand in marriage. Will you do me the honour of becoming my wife, Prudence?' Claude beamed at her, clearly expecting her to be overjoyed at his proposal.

Prue took a step backwards, her mouth opening in shock.

'I can see I have caught you unawares. You are still a good-looking woman, so it shouldn't be a surprise to you that, after a respectful period of mourning, you would attract suitors for your hand in marriage. And what better man that your late husband's brother?' He held both his arms out to the side as if to display what a fine catch he was. 'One who knows the family and the business. I believe it's what Victor would have wanted for you.'

This sentence ignited a spark of fury in Prue. *What Victor would have wanted,* she thought, fuming. That was the last thing she would *ever* do.

'No.' Prue said simply.

Claude's icy-blue eyes widened in genuine surprise. 'I, er,

well!' he flustered. 'Prudence dear, I understand if you think it's too early. If you're not ready, we can wait.'

'It's not that. I don't want to marry you, Claude. Not ever. My answer is no and will *always* remain no.' She grabbed hold of the door handle and yanked it open. 'I have work to do.'

'But...' Claude began, his eyes flashing with anger as a flush of red stained his neck and crept upwards into his cheeks. 'You won't get a better man than me, not at your age. You should grab the opportunity while you can. I don't make this offer lightly.'

'*Get out!*' Prue grabbed hold of his arm and pushed him in the direction of the open door, her heart hammering inside her. She didn't want any of this and the sooner he was gone, the better.

'You will regret not accepting me when you had the chance,' Claude snarled, attempting to jam his hat on his head but almost losing his balance as Prue, still holding his arm, continued to guide him through the doorway and outside.

Prue didn't reply. She let go of his arm, turned back inside and slammed the door shut behind him, then leaned back against it as she shook with anger and shock. How dare he come here asking her to marry him? The arrogance of the man, assuming she would accept him. What was it he'd said... that he knew the family and the business. That was what this was really all about. He wanted some control over Victor's business and, through marrying her, he thought he could get it. Marriage to Victor had been bad enough, but it would be even worse to be wedded to Claude.

Prue took several deep breaths, her heartbeat gradually returning to normal. She wasn't going to let Claude upset her any further. She'd spent too many years having her life dominated by Victor and she would not let his brother take his place. She'd told him straight, made her refusal clear and now she had more important things to do, starting with preparing for this evening's meeting.

～

Prue had worked her way through half of the pile of correspondence, making notes of items to discuss at the committee meeting, when there was another knock at the front door. This one was softer, a knocking on the wood rather than using the metal door knocker. Had Claude returned to try again?

Getting up from the kitchen table, which was covered with papers, Prue marched into the hall ready to do battle and yanked the front door open, but then let out a sigh of relief when she saw her sister standing there.

'You left this in the canteen.' Thea held up Prue's green felt WVS hat, her expression quickly clouding with concern as she stared at Prue. 'What on earth's the matter?'

'I thought it was someone else at the door. I thought he'd come back.'

'Who?'

'Claude.'

'He's been here this afternoon? What did he want this time?'

'I'll tell you.' Prue ushered Thea inside and led her to the kitchen, where they sat down at the table. 'He came to propose to me.'

Thea gasped. 'What did you say?'

'No, of course!' Prue said hotly. She told her sister what Claude had said and why he'd waited till now. 'He wasn't pleased I turned him down. He said I would regret it.'

'I doubt that very much.'

'So do I. That man has a lot of gall. There was no mention

of love to try to woo me. It was his way of getting his hands on this house and to try to have some control over Victor's business. Of course Claude still thinks Jack solely inherited the business, rather than it being shared between us all. I suspect Claude thinks I'm looking after it while Jack's away in the army and so if he married me then he could help with the running of it.'

'He's a devious man,' Thea said.

Prue shook her head incredulously, 'Did he seriously think I would say yes?'

'Most certainly. Men like Claude only see things from their own point of view. They can't imagine that anyone would turn them down and not regard them as the wonderful person they believe they are.' Thea put her hand on Prue's arm. 'Don't let it upset you. He was doing it for his own benefit, not yours. You have a much happier life now. You are free. And you're more than capable of sending him away with a flea in his ear, as you have just proven.'

Prue nodded, meeting her sister's eyes. 'You're right and I'm trying not to let it bother me. I just felt so stunned, angry and horrified. I have no plans to marry again but if I did, it would *never, ever* be someone like Claude.'

'Good.' Thea smiled. 'Now I must get home and you have more work to do.' She stood up. 'I'll let myself out. See you soon.' She gave Prue a swift hug and went into the hall, closing the front door softly behind her.

Left on her own, Prue picked up a pencil and began to read through the next letter on the pile, focusing her attention on what was important, letting the unpleasant visit from Claude fade into the background where it belonged.

CHAPTER 33

Thursdays were usually Evie's day off, but not today. This was her third day looking after Matron. Thankfully, she'd been relieved to see a marked improvement in her patient when she had checked on her at seven o'clock this morning.

Evie had spent the last two nights sleeping in the neighbouring room, getting up periodically to check on her patient. Thankfully, each time the older woman had been no worse and gradually her condition had improved. Now, following nights of broken sleep and nearly forty-eight hours of being on duty, Evie felt exhausted. She was used to working long shifts, but they were punctuated with solid lengths of time off in which she could rest and recharge. Being Matron's only nurse, Evie hadn't been able to sleep for long stretches, concerned that her patient may deteriorate, so to see Matron's improved appearance this morning was a welcome boost.

'How are you feeling?' Evie asked as she drew the curtains and removed the blackout.

'Better than I was.' Matron pulled herself up into a sitting position. 'Can you adjust my pillows, please?'

Evie did as she was asked, plumping them up and then adjusting the covers as Matron lay back against them with a gentle sigh.

'I'll just take your obs.' Evie popped a thermometer under Matron's tongue and then picked up her wrist to measure her pulse.

'What does it say?' Matron asked after Evie removed the thermometer and checked the reading before replacing it in the holder containing disinfectant.

'I'm glad to say it's back to normal.' Evie smiled. 'Would you like a drink?'

'Yes, please.'

Evie poured a glass from the jug of fresh water and handed it to Matron.

'Thank you.' Matron took a long drink. 'I think I could manage some breakfast today. Some toast and jam would be lovely.'

They both knew that was a good sign. 'Once you've eaten, I'll run you a nice warm bath and change your bedding while you're bathing. Then you can rest back in bed again or sit out in the armchair if you feel able.'

Matron touched Evie's arm. 'Thank you for all you have done for me. You're a fine nurse and I've felt in safe hands these past couple of days. I know you've made sacrifices and haven't been home since Ned carried me in here.'

Evie's cheeks grew warm. 'It's been a privilege to look after you and I'm pleased to see you looking better. I've been worried about you.'

'I don't like being ill,' Matron admitted, grimacing. 'And I would far rather be doing the nursing than receiving it. Gave myself a fright out there in the courtyard. I'd woken up feeling rough and thought a bit of fresh air might help, but my legs turned to water and I suddenly found myself on the ground. I'm so grateful you and Ned found me so quickly.'

'It was Ned who saw you fall. He ran straight out to help.'

'He's a fine man.' Matron smiled at Evie. 'You have the best of husbands, Nurse Blythe.'

Evie was happy to agree. 'I am very fortunate. Now let me go and pass on the message about some breakfast for you. I'm sure you're starving after not eating for two days.'

'Toast and jam will never have tasted so good before,' Matron said with a twinkle in her eye. 'Strawberry jam, if I may be so bold.'

Later, after Matron had enjoyed her breakfast, followed by a bath and change into a clean nightdress, Evie helped her settle into the armchair rather than going straight back to bed. Propped against a pillow, a blanket over her legs, Matron let out a deep sigh of satisfaction.

'It feels wonderful to be upright again, freshly clean and able to keep awake for more than a few minutes.'

'I'm sure it does,' Evie agreed, tucking the blanket around Matron's slippered feet. 'But you must take care not to overdo it. You're still a bit wobbly on your legs.' Evie had noticed the way the older woman clung to her arm as she'd helped her to and from the bathroom.

'I know, but it's no wonder with me not having eaten while I was ill. A couple more day's rest and good food and I'll return to work.'

Evie opened her mouth to speak but then shut it again.

'You were about to say something, Nurse Blythe?' Matron said, raising an eyebrow.

Evie hesitated for a few moments before saying, 'In my opinion you'll need more than a couple of days to recover before you go back on duty. You've been poorly and your job is busy. I think if the shoe were on the other foot, then you would insist your nurses were fully fit before they returned to their job.' She bit her lip, waiting for a reprimand for contradicting Matron. But none came. Instead, Matron let out a chuckle.

'Wise words, Nurse Blythe, and you're quite right. My spirit might be ready to get back to work, but alas, my body isn't. I need to listen to it. What day is it today?'

'Thursday.'

'In that case, I shall aim to be back on the wards on Monday, Tuesday at the latest.' A look of consternation passed over Matron's face. 'Today is supposed to be your day off, isn't it?'

Evie nodded. 'It doesn't matter.'

'On the contrary. Also, you've been nursing me for the past two days straight. I'll see that you get an extra weekend off this month in return for your dedication caring for me. I'm very grateful for what you have done.'

Evie was taken aback. 'Thank you, I appreciate that, and so will Ned. Weekends off are precious.'

Matron gave a knowing nod of her head. 'I understand how important they are with the long hours nurses have to work.' Her eyes drifted to the photograph on the bedside stand. 'I was a nurse too, remember, and for more years than I care to remember.'

'Do you mind if I ask who that is in the photograph?' Evie ventured.

'Can you fetch it for me?' Matron asked.

Placing it in Matron's hands, Evie watched as the older woman traced the tips of her fingers over the man's face, staring lovingly at the image. 'This is my fiancé, Bertie. He was killed at the Battle of the Somme.'

'I'm so sorry.'

Matron looked up at Evie, her brown eyes softening. 'Such a waste of a good man. I still miss him every day.' She held the photograph against the front of her dressing gown, over her heart. 'His death changed my life in so many ways. The war not only killed him but the prospect of our life together, of a family even.' She shook her head. 'I'm one of many women who had their future stolen by that awful war.'

'Is that why you became a nurse?'

'I was nursing before Bertie died. I went out to France as a VAD nurse, thinking it would be better to be closer to him, have the chance of seeing him more often than just waiting for him to come home on leave,' Matron explained. 'It was hard and the things I saw… but I found my calling, what I should do in life. Then after the war I trained formally as a nurse and have been doing it ever since, working my way up to Matron.' She paused for a moment then asked, 'Why did you become a VAD, Evie?'

Evie's stomach jolted at the question. Memories filled her mind of what she'd had to do to train to become a VAD, taking courses in secret so that Douglas didn't find out. Once her training was complete, she had waited until he was posted overseas before she could work as a VAD in a London hospital, all the while hiding it. She'd even travelled to and from work in her own clothes in case anyone saw her and news somehow got back to Douglas or his family.

Playing for time before she answered, Evie crossed the room to get a wooden chair and bring it nearer to Matron so she could sit on it and take the weight from her legs, which had turned to jelly at the prospect of answering Matron's question truthfully.

'I always wanted to be a nurse,' Evie said as she sat down facing the older woman, 'right from when I was a little girl.'

'You never thought of going straight into nurse training rather than being a VAD?' Matron probed.

'It wouldn't have been permitted.' The words slipped out of Evie's mouth before she could stop them. Or maybe she didn't want to stop them. Perhaps it was time, now that she had moved on and was happy, to expel some of the demons of her past and stop concealing them.

'By whom? Who wouldn't allow you to follow your calling?'

'My parents – well, my mother, as my father died when I was thirteen. She didn't think it was a suitable occupation for me. She knew I could do it, that I was capable – she just felt strongly that girls from my background shouldn't pursue a vocation.'

Matron humphed. 'What did she want you to do, then?'

'Marry well!' Evie admitted.

'You mean as in, marry money?'

Evie nodded. 'And social status.'

'Well, as decent and kind a man as Ned is, I don't think he's wealthy or from the upper classes, is he?' Matron said with a raise of her eyebrow.

Evie shook her head.

'Then may I ask, how does your mother feel about you marrying him? Does she approve?'

Evie shifted in her seat. Their conversation was getting more awkward for her and she now wished she hadn't started it by asking about the photograph lying in Matron's lap. After the past two days of nursing Matron, and what her boss had shared about Bertie, Evie wanted to be honest with her. Or at least as honest as she could be — she must not reveal the truth about her and Ned's pretend marriage, because that would be a step too far.

'No, Ned's not wealthy in monetary terms, but my first

husband was.' Evie noted Matron's surprised expression. She hadn't known this about Evie but then almost nobody knew.

'You were married before?'

'To a man who my mother approved of. Douglas was very wealthy and came from a titled family but none of that made him decent or a good husband. Quite the opposite.' She drew in a slow steadying breath. 'He was cruel to me, emotionally and physically. I lost my baby after he pushed me over. He ruled my life.'

Matron's eyes were full of sympathy and she took hold of Evie's hand, giving it a gentle squeeze. 'I'm so sorry, my dear. Where is Douglas now?'

'He was killed serving in North Africa,' Evie said. 'He can't hurt me any more.' She toyed with the idea of admitting to Matron how she had faked her death to escape him and come to work here at the hospital, but decided she'd said enough. 'He would never have allowed me to work as a VAD, but after he joined the army and was away from home, I secretly took training courses. Then, after he was sent overseas, I started working as a nurse and ended up here. When Douglas was killed, I finally felt free and safe.'

'I'm glad you came here.' Matron gave Evie's hand a last squeeze before releasing it and leaning back comfortably in the arm chair. 'And you met Ned and your life changed for the better.'

Evie nodded, smiling. 'I'm very happy here. I never expected to fall in love. Then I met Ned.'

'You deserve every ounce of happiness you can find. I understand the effect of being married to a man like your late husband – my sister wed someone of that ilk. Her husband wasn't from a wealthy or titled family, but he had an unpleasant character and treated her terribly until I got her away to safety. She's free of him now and has renewed joy in her life.'

'What happened to the husband?' Evie asked. 'Did he come looking for her?'

'No, he never knew where she was. We heard from our cousin that he was run over by a lorry when he was drunk,' Matron said matter-of-factly. 'What a conversation we're having this morning! I'm feeling tired again. Would you mind reading to me for a bit?' She pointed to the book that Evie had been reading which lay on the mantlepiece with her green leather bookmark sticking out.

'Of course, I'd be delighted to. It's *Pride and Prejudice*, is that all right?' Evie got up and fetched the book.

'That will do nicely,' Matron said, clearly looking forward to it.

'Then I shall begin at the beginning,' Evie told her, smiling.

CHAPTER 34

It felt strange to Marianne to be pushing the pram, with Bea sitting up in it and Emily walking beside it, within the boundaries of RAF Great Plumstead rather than along the roads of the village. Here, all the men and women she saw were dressed in their blue uniforms and she and her daughters were the odd ones out in their civvy clothes.

Over in the distance she could see large hangars and several aeroplanes. There were khaki-coloured military vehicles moving around. A control tower, with a railing-rimmed flat roof, stood over towards where the runways must be.

Marianne knew that this was a place most of the civilian population of the village never ventured, the entrances being well guarded to stop intruders as this was an operational station with aircraft flying in and out on missions.

Marianne was here on a mission of her own – to talk to Group Captain Barlow. With the help of her WAAF friends Marge and Elspeth, who worked in the office for the Group Captain, she'd been invited to meet him. With his permission, and her visit expected, Marianne had found herself being waved through by the men on guard duty at the gate after showing her identity card. They'd then given her directions of where to go and left her to it.

She had considered letting Emily and Bea stay at home with Hettie but then decided it would be a good idea to bring them with her. They could be a reminder to the Group Captain that there were a lot of children in the country growing up with their fathers held in POW camps. The work of the Red Cross was vital in helping these men survive their captivity and that's why it was so important to raise money to keep that aid going.

Before Marianne could knock on the door of the administrative block she'd been directed to, it opened and Marge and Elspeth came out.

'Hello, we've been watching out for you,' Elspeth said in her soft Scottish accent. 'Look at you two wee girls – you get bigger every time we see you!' She directed this towards Emily and Bea, who giggled. The children knew and adored both Waafs, who visited Rookery House regularly and were always willing to play or read or do whatever Emily and Bea wanted of them.

'Do you want to leave the girls with us while you speak to Group Captain Barlow?' Marge offered. 'It will be easier for you to talk if you don't have to worry about them. We've got some biscuits from the Naafi to share.'

Marge winked at Emily and she quickly responded with, 'Yes please!'

'Are you sure?' Marianne asked. 'Won't it stop your work?'

'We'd be glad of a break,' Marge replied. 'I've typed so many letters today that my fingers are aching.'

'In that case, thank you.' Marianne decided she could always fetch her daughters as back-up if things didn't go as well with the Group Captain as she hoped and she needed to exert some persuasion.

Leaving the pram outside the block, Marianne carried Bea while they followed the Waafs inside, with Emily walking between Elspeth and Marge holding their hands. After making sure both children were settled, sitting on chairs at an empty desk and eating a biscuit each, Marianne followed Marge past desks occupied by other Waafs who were mostly typing away rapidly, then along to another room at the far end of the corridor which had the name Group Captain Barlow on a sign on the door.

'Ready?' Marge whispered.

Marianne nodded, clutching the large brown envelope she'd brought with her.

Marge knocked and waited until a deep voice called from within for them to enter.

Marge opened the door and stepped inside, saluting. 'Mrs Marianne Fordham to see you, sir.'

'Show her in, then. And can you rustle up some tea and biscuits, Taylor?' Group Captain Barlow said, using Marge's surname.

'Yes, sir,' Marge replied, ushering Marianne in and then, as she turned to go, giving her a wink.

'Mrs Fordham.' The Group Captain stood up, came around from behind his desk and shook Marianne's hand. 'Take a seat.' He gestured for her to sit on the chair in front of his desk before returning to his own seat. 'I understand you have a request for me?' He gave her a friendly smile, his thick, sandy-coloured moustache curving above his top lip.

'I do and thank you for allowing me to come and see you today. I don't know if you know, but we are organising a May Fair in the village next weekend on Saturday 22nd. It's to raise money for the Red Cross's Prisoner of War Fund.'

Captain Barlow nodded slowly. 'I'd heard there was going to be an event in aid of the Prisoner of War Fund. A very worthy cause indeed. Several of my men who flew from here are now POWs.'

'My husband Alex is a POW. His plane was shot down on a mission over Germany,' Marianne told him. 'He's told me in letters how much the Red Cross parcels and the help they give to the POWs means to him, and all the other men too. That's why we want to raise money to keep this aid reaching them.'

'So what is it that I can help you with?' he asked. 'I presume you haven't just come here to tell me there's going to be a May Fair in the village?'

Marianne laughed. 'No, I've come to ask for your help. Firstly, with your approval, could these posters be put up somewhere where lots of your airmen and women will see them and hopefully want to come along?' She slipped two posters out of the envelope and handed them across the desk.

Group Captain Barlow scanned them. 'Of course, that's no problem. I'll...' A knock at the door made him pause and call out, 'Enter.'

Marge came into the room carrying a tray with two cups of tea on it and a plate of biscuits.

'Thank you, Taylor,' the Group Captain said as Marge placed the tray on the desk and began unloading the teacups and plate. 'Could you see these are put up to encourage those off duty to attend, one in the cookhouse perhaps, the other in the Naafi?'

Marge took the posters he held out to her. 'Of course. Is there anything else, sir?'

'Not for the moment.' He waited until Marge had left and then returned his attention to Marianne. 'The posters were your first thing. What else would you like help with?'

'We, the organisers that is, were wondering if it would be

possible for your RAF Great Plumstead band to come along and play? Some musical entertainment would be quite a draw and we could have some dancing.'

He pursed his lips thoughtfully before replying, 'It would indeed. They're a talented bunch. I'll see what I can do, bearing in mind that the men of the band are serving airmen with jobs to do on the aerodrome. Their musical collaboration is in addition to their work. But since it's helping with an important cause, I will do my best. Now please, have a biscuit.' He pushed the plate towards Marianne.

She took one and gave him a grateful smile. 'Thank you very much. We appreciate your help.'

'It's a fact that any of my men flying out on missions could find themselves as POWs. A sobering reminder that "there but for the grace of God go I". We must do what we can to help those in need.' He took a biscuit from the plate and before taking a bite asked, 'Tell me what else is planned for the May Fair? I'm all ears.'

'How did you get on?' Elspeth asked when Marianne returned to their office to find each Waaf seated with a child on their lap.

'Very well. I expect Marge has told you the Group Captain asked her to put the posters up and I'm optimistic about the band. He was interested in what we're doing and the cause we are helping. How have Emily and Bea been?'

'As good as gold,' Marge said, winking at the two little girls. She had Bea on her lap while the one-year-old made marks on the sheet of paper in front of her with a pencil.

'Look at mine, Mummy.' Emily, who was sitting on Elspeth's lap, held up her paper. 'I've drawn Marge and Elspeth.'

'So you have and they look marvellous!' Marianne lifted her daughter to her feet. 'We must go home now and let Marge and Elspeth get back to work. Shall we say "Thank you" for helping?'

'Thank you,' the little girls chorused, with Emily adding, 'Marge and Elspeth!'

'Our pleasure,' Elspeth said. 'We look forward to seeing you at the fair next weekend. I'm hoping to have a proper good spin around the dance floor!'

'So am I.' Marge stood up and put Bea on the floor, who toddled over to Marianne with her sheet of paper clutched in her hand. 'We'll spread the word about it as much as we can. The more people who turn up, the more money you'll raise.'

'That's the plan,' Marianne said. 'I'll see you both there and fingers crossed we will have a band to dance to. It would really help things go with a swing!'

CHAPTER 35

It was Hettie's turn to do a shift on the Great Plumstead WI's market day stall in Wykeham. She'd caught the train into the nearby town with Gloria earlier and now the pair of them were manning the stall, which was proving highly popular as usual and not only for the goods they sold – jars of jam or vegetables grown on the WI allotment. Today, people were also bringing *them* things to sell at the May Fair.

'I've had a sort through and hope these will raise some money,' one of their regular customers said, taking some toy cars and a spinning top out of her shopping basket and holding them out to Hettie. 'I saw the poster asking for donations for the May Fair here last week and wanted to do what I could to help.'

'Thank you, we appreciate it.' Hettie took them. 'These are sure to be popular as it's so hard to find toys in the shops these days. We've had a fantastic response to our appeal for donations. Everything will be for sale at the fair's second-hand stall on Saturday. It's going to be quite a draw and raise lots of money for the Red Cross.'

The woman was pleased. 'I'm glad to do what I can for such a good cause. Right, can I have a bunch of radishes and a spring cabbage please?'

Hettie placed the toys on top of one of the already full baskets of donations underneath the stall and served the woman with her order. 'Do come along to the fair if you can. It would be lovely to see you there. The children are doing a maypole dance and there'll be another WI produce stall and lots more besides.'

'It sounds tempting.' The woman handed over the correct money for her vegetables. 'Hope to see you on Saturday then.' She put her purchases in her basket and headed off across the marketplace.

'Well,' said Gloria, 'I didn't expect we'd get as much as this.' She gestured towards the full baskets under the stall. 'Nearly every customer we've 'ad this morning 'as given us something to sell, and there's even been some who didn't buy anything from us but dropped off donations. Word about the second-'and stall has certainly got around.'

'There aren't many who aren't affected by having a family member or friend who's already a POW and any man serving overseas has a chance of becoming one. It's hard for the loved ones of POWs, not knowing how long they will be kept a prisoner for and with no opportunity of talking to them or seeing them. Marianne struggles with it. She worries about Alex,' Hettie said, ruefully. 'So it's no surprise that people want to help in whatever way they can. Giving us something to sell is a simple thing to do and a good start, and if they come along to the fair as well and buy something, all the better.'

''opefully this lot by itself will raise plenty of money and there are lots more donations back in the village. We're going to sort through it all tomorrow, pricing each item ready for Saturday,' Gloria said as another customer arrived at the stall and she stepped forward to serve her with a welcoming, 'Hello, me ducks, what can I get for you?'

The next person to approach was a smartly dressed woman with a small dog on a lead.

'What would you like?' Hettie asked.

'How much are those toy cars?' the woman asked curtly.

'We've only got jams and vegetables for sale today,' Hettie replied with a smile. 'These jars of plum are particularly…'

'I mean those!' the woman interrupted. She stepped back and pointed to the basket underneath the stall where Hettie had placed the donated toy cars. She was already taking her purse from her handbag.

Hettie glanced at Gloria, who'd finished serving her customer. Their eyes met and a twist of amusement curled the side of Gloria's mouth.

'They're donations for the May Fair in Great Plumstead and not for sale yet,' Hettie explained.

'So they will *be* for sale?' the woman asked, her tone betraying her irritation.

'Yes, on the second-hand stall at the May Fair on Saturday.' Hettie pointed towards the poster advertising the event which was pinned to the stall.

'In that case, I'll save you the bother of having to take them there and just buy them now. How much?' She opened her purse.

Hettie didn't like her attitude. 'I'm sorry but that's not possible,' she said firmly. 'You are welcome to come along to the fair on Saturday and visit the second-hand stall.'

'But someone else might get to them first!' Pink spots bloomed on the woman's cheeks. '*I* want them, for my grandson.'

'So you think it's fine for *you* to have them first and not give anyone else a chance to see them let alone buy them?'

Hettie met the woman's eyes and held them for a few seconds before the woman looked away. 'If you want them, then I suggest you make sure you're at the second-hand stall by two o'clock sharp when the fair opens. Nothing will be on sale before then. That makes it fairer for everyone – the organisers, those who gave the donations and the customers,' Hettie said in a no-nonsense tone. 'Now, is there anything you would like from our stall today?'

'A jar of blackberry and apple jam, please.' The woman checked the price card displayed beside the stack of jars, selected the correct money from her purse and handed it over to Hettie.

'Thank you.' Hettie took the money. 'Help yourself to a jar of jam and perhaps I'll see you on Saturday then?'

The woman nodded briefly, chose a jar and placed it in her basket then stalked off, her dog trotting at her heels.

Gloria let out a soft whistle. 'Some people will try to push their luck, won't they? Mind you, it shows that there's going to be a demand for these goods. There'll be customers willing to pay for them and that's all good for us raising money.' She put her arm around Hettie's shoulders. 'I must say you 'andled her so well. I ain't sure I would have been so polite.'

'We'll see if she turns up on Saturday. I'll be watching out for her.'

By the time they'd sold all their produce, made or grown by the members of Great Plumstead's WI, it was just after midday. Hettie was delighted with how things had gone as donations had continued to come in and they had a huge amount to sell. She was grateful that Prue had arranged for the baskets of second-hand goods to be picked up and transported back to Great Plumstead in the van from Wilson's Seed and Agricultural Merchants, Victor's former business which was now owned by Prue and her three grown-up children. It would have been a struggle for Hettie and Gloria to take them on the train.

At a quarter past twelve, two men from Wilson's arrived to carry the donations to their van parked in the market square.

'We'll deliver these to Great Plumstead village hall later this afternoon,' the older man said, picking up two of the packed baskets. 'Mrs Wilson said she'll meet us there at three o'clock.'

The lad accompanying him, who'd obviously left school but was still too young to be called up, took two more baskets. 'I'll come back for the others in a minute,' he said keenly before heading off to the van.

'You've had a good lot of donations,' the older man said. 'And we've got some more in the shop that staff have brought in from home.'

'That is kind of them.' Hettie gave him a smile. 'And we appreciate you taking everything back for us. We couldn't have managed on our own.'

'You're welcome.'

Once all the donations had been collected and they'd packed up the stall, Gloria said, 'How about we go and 'ave something to eat at the cafe before we head 'ome? I reckon we deserve a treat after this morning. We've been twice as busy as usual, what with all the donations coming in.'

'Good idea,' Hettie agreed. 'The next two days are going to be hectic ones so we should take a chance to have a break while we can!'

CHAPTER 36

Prue stared out through one of the village hall's tall windows, watching large raindrops slither down the glass. It had been raining all day, the rainclouds arriving overnight after a spell of fine days. With the May Fair due to take place tomorrow, she was worried that if it carried on like this, it would deter people from coming. But the weather was out of their control. There wasn't a single thing they could do about it, other than their contingency plan to hold the fair indoors.

'Prue!' She turned at the sound of her name to see Gloria looking at her, her hands on the hips of her emerald-green dress, a concerned expression on her face. 'You all right, ducks?'

'Yes, sorry, just distracted by the rain,' Prue apologised, going over to the table where Gloria, Hettie, Marianne and a few other mothers from The Mother's Day Club were gathered.

'At least it will 'elp the vegetables grow on the allotment,' Gloria said positively. 'Now what do you think of this plan for inside the 'all?' She gestured at the large sheet of paper spread out on the table. 'The band will play up on the stage of course. The refreshments and cake stalls will go near the kitchen, that makes sense.' She pointed with her scarlet-painted fingernail to two of the rectangles drawn within the larger outline of the village hall, each neatly labelled in pencil *BAND* and *FOOD*. 'The second-'and stall goes here…' Gloria continued going through each of the stalls set out along the perimeter of the hall, while Prue and the others made noises of agreement.

Next Gloria took another, smaller piece of paper from underneath the plan of the hall. 'Here's the plan of the school. In the school's 'all, we'll 'ave the maypole 'ere, leaving enough room for dancers to perform and the audience to stand around the edges. There'll be rows of seats here… and here… for those that need them, all with good views of the maypole.'

'It all looks good,' Prue said and the other ladies agreed. 'It's going to be a tighter squeeze than if we were outside, but needs must if it's like this tomorrow. Thank you for organising what goes where.' She smiled gratefully at her friend.

'It was a bit of a puzzle, fitting things in.' Gloria chuckled. 'Even if we 'ave to 'old the fair in 'ere, we'll manage, ducks.'

'Of course we will,' Hettie said. 'Now that's sorted, we need to price up the second-hand goods.' She glanced across to the line of tables where they'd already placed the many donated items, sorting them into types. 'It would be best if we each take a pile and work through it. Anyone got a preference for what they do?'

'Can I do the toys?' Gloria asked. 'Only I 'ave an idea of what they cost, 'aving got so many little'uns, not that they had many toys bought new, mind you. But they loved 'aving a look in the shop windows.'

'Of course,' Prue agreed. Gloria was a devoted mother to Dora, who was three, but she sorely missed her five older children who'd been evacuated down to Devon and still lived there. They were in regular contact by letter but it wasn't the same.

'Marianne, would you do the clothes?'

'Yes, happy to.'

'Hettie, you'd know about the kitchen things.'

'Agreed. And I already have my eye on a couple. If they don't get sold to someone else then they're being bought by me for Rookery House.'

'Annie, will you do the books? I know you're one of our most voracious readers.'

After Prue had assigned everyone with a task, they got to work.

Picking up a small vase from her section of bric-a-brac items, Prue wondered what price she should give it. It was a nice-looking thing made of emerald-green glass and perfect for displaying flowers like primroses or violets. Would three shillings be too dear or too little?

'Is three shillings too much for this?' Prue asked Hettie who was working on the pile of kitchenware items next to her.

Hettie took it in her hand and turned it about. 'Try three and see. If it's too much and hasn't sold towards the end of the fair, then we can always reduce the price. We want to raise as much money as possible. Some things will be more popular than others and it depends what people will pay for them. I reckon the toys will sell quickly. I told you about the woman wanting those toy cars from us at the WI stall?'

'Let's hope she comes tomorrow and buys them. Gloria's going to put a suitable price on them. Reducing the prices later in the day if we need to is a splendid idea,' Prue agreed. 'We need to sell as many of these things as we can. Three shillings it is for this vase, then.' She wrote *3s.* on one of the little tickets she'd made by cutting up a cardboard cereal packet. She threaded a length of cotton through a hole punched in the labels with a pencil, then tied it around the vase.

By late afternoon, everything had been priced and left in boxes to either be displayed on the stall here in the hall tomorrow or, if the rain stopped, on the village green outside. One way or another, they would be ready for customers to buy.

'If all of this lot sells, it will earn a good few pounds for the Red Cross,' Prue said, surveying the priced goods. 'I find it especially heartening to make money from things people don't want any more.'

'Roll on tomorrow,' Gloria said, gleefully rubbing her hands. 'We'll 'ave a rush of eager customers beating their paths to this stall. Just you wait and see!'

CHAPTER 37

Marianne woke early on Saturday morning and lay still, listening. From her left came the soft sounds of her two daughters sleeping, Bea in her cot and Emily in her little bed, their gentle breathing the only noise Marianne could hear. There was no splatter of raindrops dashing against the glass windowpane as there had been when she'd woken up yesterday. Could the rain have stopped? She turned back her covers, slipped out of bed and padded over to the window. She made a small gap to the side of one curtain and then pulled the blackout away just enough so that she could peep out. To her relief, the rain and heavy, gunmetal grey clouds had gone, replaced by a fresh-washed blue sky, the May sunshine turning the world into a much brighter place than it had been on Friday, when their hopes of holding the May Fair outside today appeared already to be dashed.

She felt her shoulders relax. The May Fair could be held outside, after all. There'd be no need to squash everything into the village hall and have the maypole dancing over at the school. With the rain gone, everything could be together on the village green. Furthermore, people wouldn't be put off coming along by the bad weather. Marianne was hopeful the fair would now be able to raise the most money possible.

After letting the blackout and curtain fall back in place, Marianne returned to her bed as it was too early to get up and she didn't want to wake the girls by moving around. Instead, she would lie quietly and think through the day ahead, preparing herself for what would be a busy time.

∼

The green was a hive of activity. Members of The Mother's Day Club, along with volunteers from the Scouts and Girl Guides, had carried the fold-up tables out of the village hall and set them up for the various stalls.

Marianne was grateful that her girls were being looked after by Sylvia, Gloria's landlady, who'd offered to care for them with Gloria's daughter Dora, and bring them along to the fair later. Otherwise, it would have been impossible for Marianne to put her all into getting things ready.

'This is the last one for the second-hand stall,' a Scout said, stacking a cardboard box with the others that he and other Scouts had carried outside from the hall.

'Thank you, that's perfect,' Marianne told him and he dashed off to where Prue was calling for volunteers to collect the maypole from the school.

'It's a good job we've got the Scouts and Guides helping us,' Hettie, who was running the stall with her, said, peering into a box. 'Their legs are a lot younger than mine, better for them to do the running about. Right, let's get started setting up the stall. How about if we have toys there?' She pointed towards the far end of the three tables they'd decided they needed on account of having so much to sell. 'Then books, bric-a-brac, kitchenware and so on with clothes at this end?'

'Sounds good,' Marianne agreed. 'Shall we start with putting out the toys?'

They got to work, displaying the various items attractively so that potential customers could see what they had, in the hope they would sell as much as possible.

Elsewhere on the green, other Mother's Day Club members were setting up stalls, some with fresh produce from the WI allotment or from home gardens which had been donated. A group of Girl Guides were preparing games like hoopla and magnet fishing.

The arrival of the maypole carried by Scouts and Guides caused a stir, many people stopping to watch as it was placed in position and erected on its stand, the colourful ribbons of red, blue, yellow and green wound tightly about it.

'I used to love maypole dancing,' Hettie said. 'It was beautiful how the coloured ribbons wove into patterns around the pole as we danced. And I liked not having to hold any boys' grubby hands either, not like in other country dances we had to do.' She chuckled. 'I remember the teacher giving me a right telling off for refusing to dance with one boy, but he had the filthiest hands and so I didn't want to hold them!'

'I don't blame you,' Marianne said. 'What happened? Did you get your way?'

'No, I still had to do it.' Hettie made a face. 'But I gave my hands a thorough wash afterwards!'

As the time drew near for the fair to begin, Marianne could feel a sense of anticipation in the air. She'd noticed plenty of glances towards their second-hand stall from people passing by as they set up. And the band had arrived from RAF Great Plumstead and were now seated underneath the wide boughs of the horse chestnut tree, which was in blossom, its candlelike white and pink blossoms standing out against the fresh green leaves. An area had been roped off near the band for anyone wanting to dance.

'She's here!' Hettie hissed, gesturing towards where some people stood waiting on the edge of the green.

'Who?' Marianne asked.

'The woman I told you about who wanted to buy those toy cars while I was volunteering at the WI stall at the market. The lady in the pale blue jacket.'

'Let's see if she comes straight here as soon as the fair's declared open.'

'Perhaps she'll run! She was so desperate to have them.' Hettie's eyes twinkled mischievously. 'She might not be the only one who wants them, though. I've seen quite a few people glancing their way.'

'Toys like that are hard to come by now,' Marianne said. 'I...'

She stopped mid-sentence as Prue called out a loud 'Hello!', grabbing everyone's attention before she declared the May Fair open.

'Brace yourself,' Marianne warned Hettie and they laughed together as the first of their customers – the lady in the pale blue jacket – hurried over.

CHAPTER 38

Matron had kept her word and Evie was now enjoying her extra weekend off. This morning she'd caught up on a few tasks that she hadn't had time to do in the week while working long shifts, though Ned didn't try leaving all the domestic jobs for her as some husbands might. He did his share and between them they made a good team.

A welcome bonus of being given this weekend off was that Evie and Ned could go to the May Fair. As they walked towards the village green arm in arm, Evie could see it was already in full swing. The sound of chatting and laughing combined with toe-tapping music from the band filled the air and she noticed there were several couples on the makeshift dance floor, including Elspeth and Marge dancing with fellow RAF men.

'Would you care to join me?' Ned asked, proffering his hand.

'I'd love to.'

Ned led her into the roped-off area and they joined in with the others.

'We've never danced outside before,' Evie said. 'It's usually in the hallway at the hospital.' She recalled how it had been at the dancing after the hospital's Christmas Day tea when she'd agreed to step out with Ned. Now look at them, effectively married and living in their new home in the old grooms' rooms.

'There's no bunch of mistletoe to get caught kissing under here, though,' Ned grinned.

Evie glanced up into the branches of the horse chestnut tree, which shaded the dance area. 'No, I can't see any – what a shame,' she joked. 'But you don't need any permission to kiss me.'

'Then how can I resist?' Ned brought her to a halt and kissed her.

'Nurse Blythe!' A soft Scottish voice made Evie jump and she spun around to see Matron Reed standing on the other side of the rope, a beaming smile on her face as she looked at them. 'And Ned. I'm glad you're here. Would you join me for some refreshments, tea and cake? I'd like to treat you both, to thank you for what you did for me while I was ill.'

It took Evie a moment to find her voice. Seeing Matron here and out of her uniform was quite the surprise, and a pleasing one. She was wearing a pretty yellow flowery dress, a blue fine-wool jacket and a straw hat with a jaunty feather decorating it. And she looked and sounded so friendly, nothing like her usual strict manner.

'We were both glad to help you – really there's no need to treat us. We wanted to look after you,' Evie said.

'I know, but I *want* to thank you. So will you join me?' Matron asked. 'Please?'

Evie grinned. 'Of course, we'd be delighted, thank you.'

'It will be a pleasure,' Ned added.

Walking together over to where the refreshments were

being served, Matron asked, 'Have you had a look at the second-hand stall yet?' She gestured to what looked like the most popular stall, going by the number of people crowding around it. 'I bought a lovely brooch there.' She opened her handbag and brought it out to show them. 'Reminds me of one my mother used to have.'

'That's beautiful. No, we haven't looked at it yet,' Evie said. 'We went straight onto the dance floor. Couldn't resist the music.'

'It is rather good,' Matron agreed. 'I spotted Mr White earlier. Perhaps he and I should have a dance after we've had our tea. He's very light on his feet.'

Evie smiled inwardly, remembering how Matron had whisked the head gardener around in rather a fast foxtrot after the Christmas Day tea. She wasn't sure if he would want to repeat the experience.

Reaching the refreshments stall, they joined the end of the queue and found themselves just behind Thea, George and Betty.

'Evie!' George spotted her and threw his arms about her legs, hugging her tightly. 'We miss you.'

'I miss you too.' Evie crouched down and returned his embrace and then shared one with Betty too.

'Hello, Evie, Ned and... Matron,' Thea greeted them warmly. 'I almost didn't recognise you out of uniform. You look very smart today.'

'You're so kind. It feels good to be wearing my own clothes for a change,' Matron admitted. 'Most days I only have need of my uniform or nightgown. But that's the nature of the job and I wouldn't have it any other way. Still, it's lovely to have the afternoon off and come here. I'm treating these two fine young people for helping me.' She gestured towards Evie and Ned. 'Ned rescued me after I collapsed and

Nurse Blythe took care of me day and night while I recovered.'

'Sorry to hear you've been unwell,' Thea said. 'It sounds like you had the best of care.'

Matron nodded. 'I did. I couldn't have wished for better.'

The queue shuffled forwards. 'Right, we must decide what we'd like to have.' Matron cast her eye over the table where there was a fine selection of cakes on offer.

'Hettie made the Norfolk shortcakes and apple cake,' Thea said. 'Evie will know how delicious they always are.'

Matron closely examined Hettie's baking. 'They do look tasty. Shall we have a mixture of these?' she asked, turning to Evie and Ned.

'I'd enjoy them,' Ned said. 'That would be a real treat.'

Matron nodded. 'Then that's what we'll have, along with cups of tea.'

A short while later, seated at a small table, Matron asked, 'Are you settled in at your new home?'

'I think so.' Evie glanced at Ned, who mumbled in agreement as his mouth was full of apple cake. 'It feels cosy and we're very happy there.'

'I'm pleased to hear that. If my nurses have a good home life, it reflects well in their work. Nursing's a demanding job and it can take its toll on you. I'm sure having Ned by your side helps when you've had a hard day.' Matron's eyes met Evie's and a look of genuine affection passed between them.

'It does help – I'm very lucky to have Ned.' Evie put her hand on Ned's arm. Since she'd told Matron about her marriage to Douglas and how badly she'd been treated, Evie had sensed a softening in the older woman's attitude towards her. There was understanding and support there and Evie found it heartwarming that the older woman clearly cared for her. And although she knew Matron would not accept sloppy or less than excellent nursing from Evie and would chastise her about it should it occur, Evie felt sure she could now go to Matron for help if she needed it – whereas before she wouldn't have dared.

'Would you like to come and see our home?' Ned offered. 'Have a meal with us one day when we're both not working? We'd love to show you around.'

'I'd like that very much,' Matron replied. 'Thank you.'

How things can change, Evie thought. Not long ago she'd never have imagined wanting, or feeling happy about, Matron coming to visit. But now, Evie was glad Ned had thought to invite the older woman and Evie would genuinely welcome her into their home, not just as her boss, but as a valued colleague and even, perhaps, a new friend.

CHAPTER 39

The hour since the fair opened had passed in a blur. Marianne and Hettie had been kept busy as the second-hand stall was like a magnet, drawing in customers of all ages, each one eager to see and buy the wide variety of things they had on offer. As they'd expected, the toys and clothes had been especially popular and had sold quickly, snapped up by keen buyers.

Now as Marianne rearranged what they had left, moving things to fill in gaps and keep the display looking good, she could see how much their stock was depleted. She wished they had more donations in reserve to replenish the table.

'We could have done with double the number of donations to sell,' she said to Hettie in a quiet voice, as customers milled in front of their tables. 'I thought we had more than enough, but it's just flown off the stall. We could have sold some things several times over. I honestly thought those two women were going to come to blows over that spinning top. If you hadn't intervened, Hettie, I think they might have.'

Hettie tutted. 'Over a toy spinning top as well. I suppose it's a sign of how hard it is to get such things these days. We've done well and are still selling. I...' She halted as a woman was ready to pay for what she'd selected, so Hettie stepped forward and served her.

'Hello Marianne,' a familiar voice said.

Marianne looked up to see Grace Barker from the village grocer's shop standing in front of the stall.

'Hello! Good to see you here.'

'I wanted to come along and support the fair as it's raising money for an important cause.' Grace's eyes met Marianne's, a look of understanding passing between them as they both had loved ones being held as Prisoners of War. In Grace's case, it was her son, Robert.

'Have you heard anything more from him?' Marianne asked, knowing how desperate Grace was to hear any word. They'd often spoken about it when Marianne was in the shop. Unlike Alex, who was being held prisoner by the Germans, Grace's son had been captured by the Japanese in the Far East and news from those prisoners was sporadic.

'Nothing more.' Grace's eyes were full of misery. 'I keep on hoping that today or tomorrow might be the day we get a letter in the post from him. We've got to keep positive.'

Marianne reached across the table and touched Grace's arm. 'We do. And something like this to help the POWs feels worthwhile. I know the money we'll raise today is just a drop in the ocean of how much it costs the Red Cross to send out parcels, but every penny counts.'

Marianne just wished they'd had more to sell. Or perhaps there were other fundraising ideas she could explore. It was something she was determined to do – to help Alex, and all the POWs, in any way she could.

CHAPTER 40

'I can't remember the last time I had a go at that,' Ted said, watching the game being run by some Scouts. 'It's too many years ago.'

'Then we should remedy that right now.' Hettie steered him towards the hoopla game, her arm through his.

She was having a break from the second-hand stall now that their stock was so depleted and could be overseen by just one person. When Ted had arrived, Marianne had insisted that Hettie have a stroll around with him and she'd agreed. There was plenty to see and do and if she spent the entire time serving at the stall, then she would miss out. Besides, it was lovely to enjoy the fair with Ted.

'Would you like a go, sir?' a Scout asked as they approached. 'It's five hoops for a shilling and if you throw a hoop around a pole,' he pointed towards the short poles stuck in the ground, 'then you win a prize. One of these.' He pointed to a nearby table where there was a random assortment of prizes that the Scouts had brought along with them, from tomato seedlings in pots, to a knitted tea cosy and, Hettie noticed, a rather pretty bone china cup and saucer decorated with pink rosebuds.

'I'll have five hoops,' Ted said, fishing into his jacket pocket and handing over some coins to the Scout, who gave him the rubber hoops in return.

'You must stand behind the line, here.' The Scout stood on the white chalky line that had been drawn across the grass about ten feet in front of the poles and mimed throwing a hoop. 'Best of luck.'

'Thank you,' Ted said. 'I'm going to need it! It's been a long time since I last played and I wasn't much good then.'

Hettie watched as Ted threw his first hoop, which fell clear of all the poles.

He groaned. 'Missed!'

Each of the next three hoops failed to even glance against a pole, let alone land around one.

'The years have not improved my hoopla throwing skills.' Ted chuckled.

'One left to go, so give it your all. Good luck!' Hettie encouraged him.

'Here goes.' Ted launched the last hoop. It flew away from him high over the poles and landed with a plop around the furthest one.

'You did it!' Hettie patted Ted's arm. 'Well done.'

Ted grinned, a look of astonishment on his face. 'Must have been the luck working. My heart's beating like I just won the hundred yard dash!'

'Congratulations,' the Scout said. 'Please choose a prize.'

'I'll let Hettie do that.' Ted gestured for her to take her pick from the prizes on offer.

'In that case, I'll have the teacup and saucer please,' Hettie said.

The Scout handed them to Hettie.

She turned to Ted and gave him a beaming smile. 'Thank you for winning me these. They're beautiful and will always remind me of your daring hoopla throw,' Hettie said, admiring the cup and matching saucer.

'It was a rare event indeed.' Ted held out his arm for Hettie to take. 'Shall we have a dance? I promise I'm better at dancing than throwing hoops.'

'That sounds lovely.' Hettie placed her prize inside her spacious handbag, wrapping each item neatly in the spare headscarf she kept in there, then took Ted's arm.

As they walked towards the dance floor area, Hettie felt herself glowing with happiness. She was a fortunate woman, with her wonderful home and friends at Rookery House. Her unexpected friendship with Ted had enriched her life further. Everything they did together brought her joy, be it going to the pictures or a day out in Norwich. Now they were about to add dancing to their experiences together and what better place to do that than at the May Fair?

CHAPTER 41

Prue watched as Hettie and Ted waltzed around the makeshift dance floor, the pair of them looking so happy. It was lovely to see them together and enjoying themselves. She was delighted with the way so many of the residents of Great Plumstead, of all ages, had come to the fair this afternoon. It was turning into a fine social occasion and a chance for everyone to have fun.

As the band finished their number, Prue hurried forwards and spoke to the RAF sergeant who'd been playing the trumpet and stood front and centre stage, clearly their most accomplished musician.

'We're going to start the maypole dancing in a few minutes, so if you'd like to take a break, now would be the time. There's some complimentary tea and cake waiting for you all over at the refreshments stall. Please have some,' Prue told him.

'Thank you very much. We'll enjoy that,' the sergeant replied. 'Shall we play again once the maypole dancing's over?'

'If you're happy to do so.' Prue gave the other men in the band a smile of appreciation.

'We are. This is all good practice, as well as a lot of fun. Thank you for inviting us.'

Leaving the band to get some refreshments, Prue went to the centre of the stalls area on the green and, after taking a deep breath, called out in her loudest voice, 'Hello! Can the maypole dancers please make their way to Miss Carter, ready to dance?'

A wave of excited chatter filled the air as the children hurried over to their teacher.

'Come on,' Nancy said, rushing across to Prue, 'I don't want to miss this. Marie and Joan 'ave been talking about nothing else for days.'

Prue didn't want to miss it either. Having evacuees Nancy and her children lodge with her had been like having a second family. She was as desperate to see Marie and Joan dancing the maypole as she would have been to watch her own children.

Prue followed her friend to where other mothers and fairgoers were gathering, leaving plenty of room for the dancers to perform.

'Look at them – they're both so excited about it,' Prue said, glancing over to where Marie and Joan were waiting with the other children gathered by their teacher. 'I remember Alice and Edwin both enjoyed maypole dancing, but not Jack. He didn't like it, or the country dancing they had to do.'

'I never got to do maypole dancing at my school,' Nancy said. 'Though I think I'd 'ave liked it. Here they go.'

The audience fell silent as the children moved into position, forming in a wide circle around the maypole, alternating boy, girl. Each of them held one of the long red, blue, yellow or green ribbons connected to the top of the wooden pole. As they waited for the signal to begin, only the sound of swallows and house martins chattering as they flitted overhead could be heard. Then Miss Carter started the music on the gramophone that had been brought out from the school and, with four claps of her hands, counted the dancers in.

Prue smiled as she watched the children skipping round the maypole, her foot tapping to the beat of the music. Round and round they went, moving in and out of each other. As the dance progressed, the ribbons wove around the wooden pole making a colourful pattern, which brought exclamations of delight from the audience. At the end of the gramophone record, Miss Carter signalled for the children to turn ready to dance in the opposite direction, then set the music going again and counted them in. This time, the dancing undid the ribbons until they were all hanging free once more. Finally, the dancers curtsied or bowed and the audience broke into an enthusiastic round of applause.

'That was marvellous!' Nancy exclaimed, waving madly to her girls.

'Yes!' Prue agreed. Having the maypole dancing at the fair was such a wonderful addition. Not only did it involve the children, but it was a link to the past. Many of the audience, like Prue herself, had danced around it when they were at school and Prue felt comforted to have the tradition continue despite the turmoil and uncertainty of living in a country at war.

After all the maypole dances were over, Prue was on her way to check on the stalls to make sure everything was running smoothly and see if anything was needed when she heard her name called by a familiar voice. She turned around to see Clemmie walking towards her.

'Hello Prue! Wasn't the dancing marvellous? I'm so glad I got here in time to watch it. The children must have practised diligently to get it spot on.'

'Hello, Clemmie,' Prue greeted her friend warmly. 'I didn't realise you were here. It's good of you to come.'

'I would have been here sooner, only Anthony arrived home unexpectedly,' Clemmie explained. 'Do you have a moment?'

'Yes of course – is everything all right?'

Clemmie put her hand on Prue's elbow and steered her away from where they might be overheard. When they reached the edge of the fair area, she said, 'It is.' Prue detected relief in her voice. 'I'm delighted to say that all is well and as it should be. In fact, I would go as far as saying it's *better*, because after our little "meeting" in York, Anthony and I have come to an understanding. He now knows that I've been aware of what he has been doing all these years and that there is a boundary he must not cross. He nearly did so with the latest one and, although he's told me the intentions I uncovered were much more on her side than his, it has shaken him. I think because he wasn't serious about her at all. My husband will be a great deal more careful in future about who he has his casual flings with.'

'I'm glad to hear that,' Prue said. She marvelled at her friend's handling of her husband's behaviour, managing to keep her focus on the larger picture of securing her and the Hall's future, and the continuation of everything else she'd worked so hard for.

'There's more. As a gesture of repentance, Anthony was happy to agree to my suggestion that he make a sizeable donation to today's fundraising for the Prisoner of War fund.'

Clemmie took an envelope out of her handbag. 'There is a cheque in here for one hundred and fifty pounds payable to the Red Cross POW fund.' She handed it to Prue.

Prue was lost for words for a few moments before finding her voice. 'Thank you, that's wonderful! Please pass on our thanks to his Lordship.'

'I will. Right,' Clemmie looked around her. 'Shall we have a wander around the stalls?'

CHAPTER 42

'I can't believe how much we made today,' Marianne said, staring at the piles of coins sorted out into farthings, ha'pennies, pennies, thrup'nny bits, sixpences, shillings, florins and half-crowns on Prue's kitchen table. The cheque from Lord Campbell-Gryce lay beside them. 'Sixty-eight pounds, five shillings and three pence! Astonishing. And we must add his Lordship's generous donation on top.'

'Just goes to show what can be done,' Gloria said, smiling.

After the fair had finished and everything was cleared up and packed away, Gloria and Marianne had gone home with Prue to count the takings. First, they'd sorted the coins each stall had made into the different denominations, then counted them, checking and double-checking the amounts of each before adding it all up to give them a total.

'And there's no surprise which stall earned the most.' Prue pointed towards the largest pile.

'The second-hand stall!' Marianne and Gloria chorused and then both burst out laughing.

'If we'd had even more donations to sell, they would have

gone,' Marianne said. 'Nearly everything went apart from a few odd things that I'm not sure anyone would want. The toys and clothes were so popular. Makes me wonder if we could do more, maybe have a second-hand stall sometimes at Wykeham market day, like the WI produce one. It might raise money all year round.'

'Would you get enough donations to stock it?' Gloria asked.

'I don't see why not. We only collected them for the fair over a short time. People might have more to give and we could spread the word further.'

'There would only be limited space on a stall,' Prue advised. 'We would have to transport the things there each time and need somewhere to store them. On this occasion it was fine to keep them in the village hall for a few days just before the fair but I think there would be objections to using it for long-term storage.'

'We should start a second-hand *shop*,' Marianne joked. 'But that would cost money as we'd have to pay rent. Perhaps we could just hold a sale twice a year in the hall instead. That at least would work.'

'Sounds like a good idea,' Gloria agreed. 'Today has showed us there are customers willing to buy second-hand things, so we just need to do it in a way that's manageable.'

'Wait!' Prue looked thoughtful. 'There *might* be another way. Do you think if we found a shop, but didn't need to pay anything to use it, then we would have enough volunteers to run it and donations to fill it?'

Marianne looked at Gloria and they both nodded.

'We'd both volunteer and plenty more would,' Marianne said. 'But where are we going to find a shop to use for nothing?'

'Leave it with me.' Prue gave a mischievous smile. 'I will

make some enquiries tomorrow and let you know. And if something can be found, then I shall volunteer to help as well.'

Marianne sat back in her chair and smiled. 'That sounds promising, but honestly, if it doesn't work out, then we will have some more second-hand sales here in the village. One way or another, we'll keep raising money for the POW fund.'

CHAPTER 43

Wykeham – late June

'Have you seen the queue?' Marianne stared out of the shop's bay window. 'It's snaking across the market square! I never expected this.'

Hettie joined her by the window and peered out. 'Nor did I, but all those customers will give us a good start and hopefully raise lots of money.'

Marianne smiled at her dear friend, who'd been a stalwart supporter of this new venture, along with Prue and Gloria, who were also volunteering here today to open Wykeham's new Red Cross Prisoner of War Fund shop.

They'd come a long way from their second-hand stall at the May Fair last month and had now set up the small shop overlooking Wykeham's market square, stocking it with donated goods plus some new hand-made items. Members of The Mother's Day Club had used oddments of fabric left over from dressmaking to make plush toy rabbits and dolls. They'd even knitted dishcloths from cotton yarn to sell.

None of this would have been possible without Prue, Marianne thought, looking over to where she and Gloria were making a few last-minute adjustments to their displays of goods. It was Prue's generosity that had given them this shop. It was part of Wilson's Seed and Agricultural Merchants premises and had been used as an office. Prue had seen its potential and had had it rearranged, relocating the office to elsewhere in the building so that they could have the space for the shop. With a door opening out onto the market square and a bay window with a wide windowsill for displaying their wares, it was perfect. There was even a small storage room at the back. Best of all, it was rent and rate free so that every single penny they raised would go straight to the Red Cross's Prisoner of War Fund.

Marianne had pinned some leaflets on the wall that she'd been sent by the Red Cross, explaining all about the parcels so customers could know exactly where the money they spent in the shop would be going. She'd also taped a poster on the window showing a soldier clutching a POW parcel. It was an emotive reminder for customers of why the shop was there.

'It's ten o'clock and time to open for business.' Gloria came over and looked out of the window, her eyes widening. 'They ain't all going to fit in 'ere at once! We'll 'ave to limit the numbers coming in. What do you think?' She peered around the shop. 'Eight at a time?'

'No more than that,' Prue agreed, joining them. 'Our customers must have room to move about and look at the goods on offer. Right, this is it, ladies. We've done a sterling job getting it organised and set up and now it's time to open for business. Marianne, will you do the honours?'

'I'd love to.' Marianne took a last look around, marvelling

at the amount of donations they'd received as word spread about what they were doing. Despite her confidence after the May Fair, she'd been worried they might have already had all that could be donated but plenty more had come in. Some of the donations were even better than before, like the doll's bed and child's desk and chair set. Marianne walked to the shop door and, as she put her hand to the doorknob, she smiled back at her friends, who stood watching her.

'Remember to count eight in and stop the next one,' Hettie reminded her, 'otherwise we'll end up packed in here like sardines.'

Marianne opened the door and a cheer went up from the waiting crowd.

'Good morning, everyone,' Marianne greeted them. 'It's wonderful to see you all here at the grand opening of this Red Cross shop. We have a fine selection of goods for you to choose from, but because space is limited inside, we will only be able to let eight customers in at a time, so there's enough room for you to browse comfortably.' She waved the first women in the queue forwards into the shop, counting as they went by before putting up her hand to halt the ninth. 'If you'd wait here for a few minutes please, and then you'll be next in.'

The woman smiled and put her shopping basket on the ground to happily await her turn.

Marianne stepped back just inside the shop door, from where she had a good view of what was happening with the customers who'd been admitted.

The set of Snow White and the Seven Dwarves toys, priced at £2. 5s., had been snapped up. The smartly dressed woman who'd bought them was getting envious looks from several of the other women who clearly would also have liked them.

It was a very good start, Marianne thought. Long may it continue.

Prue, Gloria and Hettie were kept busy serving and taking money. Each time Marianne let customers out and admitted new ones, she noticed those still waiting in the queue were curious to see, and often admire, what had been bought.

By the end of the first half hour of opening, all the larger items, including the dolls' bed, which they'd priced at £2.10s. and the child's desk at £3, had all gone. As the morning progressed, the plush fabric dolls sold out and they would have sold many more if they'd had any. Thankfully, no one quibbled at the prices. As they had set up the shop, there'd been a lot of discussion over how much to charge, considering the items were mostly second-hand. They didn't want to sell them too cheaply as they wanted to raise as much money as they could but nor did they want to overcharge. Marianne was delighted to see that they seemed to have got it right and that all the customers appeared satisfied.

'Come again and please spread the word that we need donations to keep the shop running,' Marianne said, opening the door to let another happy customer out. It was a message she'd said to each one as they left because they needed more goods coming in, to sell along with the hand-made items.

'I will.' The woman smiled at Marianne. 'My granddaughter is going to be delighted with this rabbit.' She gestured at the soft toy lying in her wicker shopping basket. 'It's lovely.'

Marianne returned her smile. 'We look forward to seeing you again soon.'

By the time they shut the shop at four o'clock, the steady stream of customers had almost completely depleted their shop's stock, with very little left to sell. Had they had more, it would have gone too.

'What a day!' Hettie said, her cheeks flushed and her eyes bright behind her round glasses. 'I think we can safely say it's been a great success.'

'It 'as, and so busy,' Gloria agreed. 'My feet are aching.' She glanced down at her high-heeled, white peep-toed shoes. 'I'm used to wearing these but maybe they ain't the best thing for being a shopkeeper in.' She let out a throaty laugh. 'But all for a good cause, eh? How much have we taken, Prue?'

Prue, who was standing behind the little counter, counting the money, finished totalling up the coins stacked in denominations in front of her. 'Forty-nine pounds, seven shillings and five pence! An excellent day's takings.'

'That's wonderful!' Hettie said.

'And almost enough to pay for *a hundred parcels*!' Marianne exclaimed, her eyes filling with tears of joy.

Gloria put her arm around Marianne's shoulders and hugged her. 'This is only the start, ducks. Now we ain't just got things on sale for an afternoon at a fair. Our shop is 'ere to stay for as long as we need it to be, ain't that right, Prue?'

'Absolutely,' Prue agreed. 'The shop will remain open and we'll keep making things and asking for donations.'

'I've enjoyed myself,' Hettie said. 'We've had a busy few weeks but it has been worth it.'

Marianne looked at her dear friends who'd embraced this new venture, along with many other women from The Mother's Day Club, who would take it in turns to run the shop on days it was open. Together they were all making a difference, their strong friendships and spirit helping to care for those loved ones far from home. Today was just the beginning and Marianne felt optimistic about the future.

Suddenly she saw Alex in her mind's eye, smiling as ever. Maybe she'd spot him for real in the next edition of *The Prisoner of War* or maybe she wouldn't. All she knew for sure was that he would be back with her one day and, until then, she'd be working hard for him and keeping his family safe.

Marianne had a clear purpose now and could see her path ahead until the time when the war ended and her beloved Alex came home at last.

Dear Reader,

I hope you enjoyed reading *A Joyful Springtime at Rookery House* and catching up with Evie and Marianne again in this spring story.

Prue, Thea and Hettie and the other residents of Great Plumstead will return next in *New Beginnings at Rookery House*.

I love hearing from readers – so please do get in touch via:

Facebook: be friends on **Rosie Hendry Books,** or join my private readers group - **Rosie Hendry's Reader Group**
X (Twitter): @hendry_rosie
Instagram: rosiehendryauthor
Website: **www.rosiehendry.com**

On my website, you can sign up to get my newsletter delivered straight to your inbox, with all the latest on my writing life, exclusive looks behind the scenes of my work, and reader competitions.

If you have the time and would like to share your thoughts about this book, do please leave a review. I read and appreciate each one as it's wonderful to hear what you think. Reviews also encourage other readers to try my books.

With warmest wishes,

Rosie

IF YOU ENJOYED A JOYFUL SPRINGTIME AT ROOKERY HOUSE…

It would be wonderful if you could spare a few minutes to leave a star rating, or write a review, at the retailer where you bought this book.

Reviews don't need to be long – a sentence or two is absolutely fine. They make a huge difference to authors, helping us know what readers think of our books and what they particularly enjoy. Reviews also help other readers discover new books to try for themselves.

You might also tell family and friends you think would enjoy this book.

Thank you!

HEAR MORE FROM ROSIE

Want to keep up to date with Rosie's latest releases?

Subscribe to her newsletter on her website.
www.rosiehendry.com

Subscribers get Rosie's newsletter delivered to their inbox and are always the first to know about the latest books, as well as getting exclusive behind the scenes news, plus reader competitions.

You can unsubscribe at any time and your email will never be shared with anyone else.

ACKNOWLEDGMENTS

A huge thank you to all my readers who have taken the Rookery House books and characters to their hearts.

Thanks to the fantastic team who help me create the books — editor, Catriona Robb and cover designer, Andrew Brown. Also to my author friends and especially those of the Famous Five whose friendship, chats and laughs together are such a joy.

Finally, thank you to David, who supports me in all I do.

Have you met the East End Angels?

Winnie, Frankie and Bella are brave ambulance crew who rescue casualties of the London Blitz.

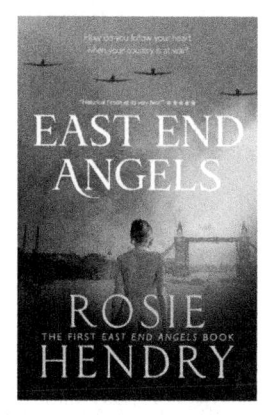

BOOK 1 - USA and Canada edition

BOOK 1 - UK and rest world English edition

Available in ebook, paperback and audiobook.

ALSO BY ROSIE HENDRY

East End Angels series
East End Angels
Secrets of the East End Angels
Christmas with the East End Angels
Victory for the East End Angels
East End Angels Together Again

Rookery House series
The Mother's Day Club
The Mother's Day Victory
A Wartime Welcome at Rookery House
A Wartime Christmas at Rookery House
Digging for Victory at Rookery House
A Christmas Baby at Rookery House
Home Comforts at Rookery House
Christmas Carols at Rookery House
A Joyful Springtime at Rookery House
New Beginnings at Rookery House (coming soon!)

Standalone
Secrets and Promises
A Home from Home
Love on a Scottish Island
A Pocketful of Stories

Rosie Hendry lived and worked in the USA before settling back in her home county of Norfolk, England, where she lives in a village by the sea with her family. She likes walking in nature, reading and growing all sorts of produce and flowers in her garden — especially roses.

Rosie writes stories from the heart that are inspired by historical records, where gems of social history are often to be found. Her interest in the WWII era was sparked by her father's many tales of growing up at that time.

Rosie is the winner of the 2022 Romantic Novelists' Association (RNA) award for historical romantic sagas, with *The Mother's Day Club*, the first of her series set during wartime at Rookery House. Her novels set in the London Blitz, the *East End Angels* series, have been described as 'Historical fiction at its very best!'.

To find out more visit **www.rosiehendry.com**

Printed in Dunstable, United Kingdom